A HAUNTING LOVE

EMILEE HARRIS

Copyright © 2021 Emilee Harris
All rights reserved.

FREE Download:

Get your FREE copy of The Commodore's Daughter, prequel to Emilee's *Currents of Love* series when you sign up for the author's mailing list at:
www.authoremileeharris.com

FOREWORD

When I met Emilee Harris almost four years ago at the InD'Scribe Con, little did I know she would become one of my favorite book friends. As a shy introvert, I'm not typically very good at making connections. I'll forever be grateful to Emilee who waved me over to join her and another author for lunch. We hit it off immediately due to her warmth and genuine kindness. I was a newer author just starting out with my first paranormal romance novel. Emily was a big champion of that now complete series, and I cherished the support.

Now, Emilee has written her own paranormal romance novel every bit as descriptive and lovely as her historical romances, and I have the honor of championing this wonderful work. *A Haunting Love* is everything the title promises. From the hauntingly beautiful scenery to a strong-minded heroine who wants nothing more

FOREWORD

than her freedom and independence, this book is vivid, fanciful, and atmospheric. Add in a dreamy, charmingly argumentative ghost, and you have a recipe for a romantic story you won't want to put down.

One thought kept occurring to me over and over as I read *A Haunting Love,* and that is, love will always find a way. This theme carries throughout the story seamlessly right through to the satisfying conclusion. You will take a ride with our heroine, Adele, as she determinedly works her way through a life that isn't always easy. Things look up when she rents a house no one else wants – a house haunted by a rough sea captain who doesn't want anyone inside his precious home. That is until he meets his match in Adele. Captain Daniels' rugged nature leads to much humorous banter between the two that will have you laughing and swooning in equal measure.

This is a story you will easily fall in love with, and I'm honored to be able to introduce it to you. Believe me, I know the paranormal, it was my first love, after all, and this story is everything you could want from the genre.

— A.D. BRAZEAU, AUTHOR OF THE
IMMORTAL KINDRED SERIES

CHAPTER 1

The sharp claw of an icy autumn breeze caught the edge of Adele's translucent black veil, whipping it about her in corkscrew fashion. Mother Nature's attempt, perhaps, to make good on Adele's unspoken desire to be rid of her misery, though this was not quite the route she hoped for. Not that she'd formed any definitive plan, which served as part of the problem. Gripping at the mass of tulle with semi-effectual fingers ensconced in their own midnight cotton sateen gloves, she wrestled with the encumbrance until the elements took pity on her and redirected the breeze, no doubt diverting their attention to a more agreeable playfellow.

Adele, now the widow Monroe, continued to rustle and fidget a moment longer before settling into her accustomed pose, mimicking the statuary interspersed amid the headstones. When seen through the open-minded lens of modern thought, one might imagine the cemetery as truly picturesque and peaceful, reminiscent of the impressionist landscapes so well received only a few decades prior. Soft light suffused the expanse before her via the brilliant palettes of late-season foliage. Summer flared in a phoenix-like death blaze before an early autumn, every leaf a second's worth of brush stroke on the greater canvas before her. Alas, Adele's thoughts could fathom no such depth of meaning. Too many earthly concerns clamored for her attention, manifesting sharply through the same surroundings that provided her only source of private calm these days.

No conveniently situated bench sat in the vicinity of her husband's grave. The quilt-block of earth appeared out of place, no longer fresh but not yet homogeneous with the more established surrounds. The effect unsettled Adele enough to keep her gaze continually swaying from side to side. Her legs ached with prolonged stillness, but she feared straying too far from the site might somehow send alarms sounding in the home of her in-laws, on whom she now found herself dependent. Shifting from one frozen foot to the other, she rubbed her hands together in front of her and stared across the gray-cobbled field. With a guilty blink, she remembered to send a cursory glance down toward the stone in front of her, a gaudy expression of what her mother-in-law considered understated elegance befitting an architect, however unrecognized he might have been.

Her mouth bobbed in an unfamiliar manner, her conscience prompting her to unburden her soul to the life partner who never once asked about her dreams and ambitions during his time on earth. As a husband, one might describe him in similar fashion to his architectural legacy: sufficient and unexceptional. A chastising breeze ruffled her black crepe hem and she shivered, nodding her acknowledgment. One must not think ill of the dead.

He met the demands placed on him and Adele never thought to encourage him toward anything greater. Her current predicament therefore stemmed as much from her doing as his. Turning toward the packed dirt of the walkway, her knees creaked as they hefted their slight burden, buried in dismal fabric, toward the cemetery gate. As much as it pained her to admit even to herself, these daily sojourns were less the proof of a grieving widow and more the only allotment of privacy for a woman crushed under the good intentions of family.

"It's not something one is ever encouraged to consider," she muttered, eyes dragging along the dirt, picking out the tiny triangles of her boot toes blinking in and out of sight beneath her hem. "A wife might die young in childbearing, but a husband ought to live into old age."

Yet here she stood, widowed after only a decade of marriage and still in the relative bloom of youth. At thirty-three, Adele exuded a child-like quality which she at times suspected hindered her independence. The meager wealth of her husband, acceptable in terms of modest beginnings meant to grow over time, stood no chance of supporting a widow and two children, the eldest barely nine years of age. Even after selling the house he built for them and nearly all their possessions, she was left with next to nothing and forced to endure the charity of her mother-in-law.

That charity weighed heavier with each passing day.

"It's unseemly," Mrs. Monroe, her mother-in-law, would cluck from the corner of the stuffy parlor where no light had been allowed to enter through the thick mourning drapes for weeks. "The widow Evans was out at a charity bake just last week, her poor husband not even six months in the grave! Can you imagine? And wearing navy! One would think she'd never cared for the dear man a day, and they were married twenty-five years!" Piteous sniffling generally ensued, accented by dabbing a starched black handkerchief to dry eyes.

Adele stretched her neck against her high collar, sucking in a deep sigh and regretting it instantly when her veil clamped over nose and mouth with suffocating force. Puffing out small mouthfuls of air and pinching the material away from her face long enough to breathe properly for the span of a few heartbeats, she exited the cemetery through a permanently ajar gate.

While not technically part of Boston proper, Newton sat close enough to provide most of the city amenities and claimed a rail route that allowed easy access to the city if desired. More often than not in recent days, Adele found herself tempted to board the rail, but not for an excursion to Boston. She wondered how far the tracks might take her and if some small cove existed along the shore which might provide a quiet retreat for herself and her children.

The wind let out a breathy laugh, propelling her along the path into town. Much like an unobservant child, it tugged at her skirts with enough ferocity to force her movement while swerving direction often enough to impede that movement with the subsequent tangling of layers. She hardly noted her entrance to town, focusing instead on maintaining an upright position while battling both veil and skirts in an attempt to slow her momentum. Luckily, not many locals chose that blustery day to linger about the streets.

Through thoroughfares and byways the wind carried her, directing every step and pushing from behind when her legs threatened to slow their pace. By the time she found refuge in an alcoved doorway, she'd quite lost her breath and leaned heavily on the exterior paneling of the building. Several moments of deep breathing ensued, one gloved hand monitoring the rise and fall of her chest and ascertaining the frantic rhythm of the heart therein before Adele declared herself sufficiently stable to take on the task of yet again rearranging the layers of crepe and tulle encasing her.

With her person set to rights, now several minutes past her initial entry into the recess, she blinked in the direction of the street, distrustful of the calm now blanketing the landscape. Hesitant to venture forth, she diverted her attention to her rescuing bower, noting the faded green quarter-sphere awning protruding out into the street from where it met the building wall above her. As she stood now underneath and further back from the protective fabric, the wording on the front evaded her. The walls beside her, sporting dark windows looking in on nothing, proved more helpful. Round about the edges like an internal frame wandered crisp lines of gold, matching the lettering slightly north of center which read: Alderman & Son Realty.

Brows ticking up, she leaned in closer to the window, spying on the other side a small collection of picture frames. One hung from the next in a vertical row, each encasing small sketches of homes. Beneath each sketch ran a short, typed paragraph with information pertaining to the number of rooms to be found in each and various additional details which might be thought to entice a future resident.

Biting her bottom lip, she glanced toward the door as though someone might charge forth at any moment and chase her away. Straightening, she purposefully recalled thoughts of life in her mother-in-law's house.

"Surely it wouldn't do any harm to inquire," she mused, leaning down to read the description of the home near the bottom of the window.

You can't afford it, a voice responded from the depths of her self-doubt.

"There's no way to know that until I ask, is there?" She asserted into the empty niche surrounding her. "Didn't mother always say 'for every pot there is a lid'?" Granted, the phrase had more to do with romantic matches in her mother's recitation, but the sentiment seemed relevant in this case as well. A brief stab of doubt returned, barely noticed as the wind, taking note of her interest in the interior of the building, gave an angry howl and asserted itself again. This show of temper, along with Adele's lack of enthusiasm to return to the house which currently acted as her home, encouraged the newly rooted idea to swiftly sprout and bloom. With a nod to herself and the addition of a smile to her features, she straightened and turned to face the door, reaching out a hand before her thoughts found an opportunity to revert to their earlier qualms.

∽

A SMALL BELL above the door announced her entry as Adele stepped over the threshold, holding tightly to the handle to prevent the heavy wooden slab from slamming against the wall. Turning to shield herself behind it, she leaned her slight weight into the wood, wrestling it back to a closed position. Once she succeeded in her endeavor, she paused in place to perform the ritual of concerted breathing and disentangling from the mummifying effects of her veil. She found little reassurance in the movements swiftly becoming a staple of her existence.

"May I help you?" came a small voice from the interior of the room.

Spinning around, her eyes darted from one side of the room to the next, over stacks of paperwork, around file cabinets, between desks, and back again until they came to rest on a figure all but hidden behind several stacks of catalogs and ledgers on a desk far too small to support them. "Oh, ah—"

"I take it you are searching for housing in or near our fine town?" The figure continued, without rising from his post.

She blinked, momentarily rendered speechless by the unnatural amplification of dull brown eyes sparsely lashed and shielded behind thick glasses. Eyes which now surveyed her top to bottom. The effect proved similar to watching a fish maneuver back and forth in its bowl. "Ah, yes, that's exactly right."

The man hopped to his feet, remaining in the space behind the desk, and held out a hand indicating she should take a seat in the chair on the other side of the workspace.

"Wesley Alderman, the son portion of Alderman and son, at your service. We have a fine selection of homes here, ma'am, I am sure we can offer you something perfectly suited. Will the space be occupied singly?" He slid a sideways glance toward her head-to-toe immersion in black as he turned slightly to pull a large catalog from its place mid-way through the stack beside him.

Her eyes widened as the tower of tomes swayed ominously, but a moment later the catalog sat in front of him, the other books rested in practiced boredom, and those brown eyes behind their twin fishbowls waited expectantly.

"Er, no, it will be myself and two children, plus a housekeeper." She narrowly prevented herself from cringing, knowing very little chance of maintaining her housekeeper, Bessie, existed but even less willing to contemplate such a plight as to admit her grave lack of funds. To rely upon her own talent alone to feed her children and maintain a home might be tantamount to a death sentence.

"Wonderful. In that case a minimum of three bedrooms... he mumbled to himself, having opened the book and begun flicking through pages.

A ticking from a side wall caught her attention. The clock, with its dull brass pendulum and fogged-over glass nevertheless reported accurate time on the sickly ivory expanse of its face. Beside the clock, giving off a much smarter appearance in gleaming polished oak with brass fittings, preened a barometer. This apparatus shone in true naval fashion, reporting air pressure and humidity with sleek, sharp pointers easily visible through a clear glass covering. Adele wondered at the odd piece. Not odd in its existence, perhaps, this was a suburb of Boston after all, but odd in its stark contrast of appearance to every other surface and item in the office.

A subtle glance around her confirmed her first impressions: dull. Every colored surface from wooden desks to wallpaper emitted the tiredness and pallor of time. The desks themselves, replete with nicks and scratches, looked ready to creak and groan on cue. Only the barometer shone with misplaced vitality. She contemplated asking about it, but Mr. Alderman chose that moment to announce his findings.

"Let's see..." He mumbled, pursing his lips. "Emery house. Four beds, large kitchen, fine garden, sea view, close to all amenities... One thousand two hundred dollars per annum." He paused in his recitation, head bobbing up and one eyebrow questioning.

Adele gave a small shake of her head, willing her cheeks not to flare. "It sounds lovely, but rather large for a widow. For maintenance purposes, you understand. Also, I can't see needing the additional bedroom at present."

"I see," he dipped his head again toward the catalog in front of him, showcasing a balding portion of his crown as he flipped to the next dog-eared page. "Well, there's New Harbor, three bedrooms, no sea view, but conveniently located near the schoolhouse, which I imagine would be of importance... Nine hundred dollars annually." Again, one caterpillar of an eyebrow crawled its way atop the frames of the man's glasses.

Her heart sank a bit and she swallowed. "It sounds lovely, but I'd hate to make any decisions in haste. I prefer to exhaust my options first. Perhaps we could compile a list from which I might choose after seeing the properties in more detail?"

He gave a quick nod and returned to the somewhat brittle ivory pages. When next he began to murmur, the sounds emitted via more subdued tones, indicating personal perusal rather than intended vocalization. "Three bedrooms, furnished. Seaside, large garden with patio, outmoded but functional kitchen… One hundred fifty dollars yearly…"

She perked up, but at the same time the man's eyes widened, which hardly seemed possible given their already magnified state, and darted up to the top of the page. "Coral Cottage. Oh, forgive me, that one won't do." He ducked his nose toward the center fold of the catalog, fingers fondling paper corners with excessive interest.

"Why not?" Adele questioned, mind already settling on the incomprehensibly low asking price. And furnished! That would save her a considerable amount of cost in outfitting a new home. In fact, she could sell most of what she'd kept from her marital home and come out ahead in the wager. It sounded too good to be true. On that note her shoulders sank. "What's wrong with the place?" She questioned outright. "The foundation? The roof? The pipes?"

The Realtor cast her a profoundly pained expression,

the musculature of his features moving in a dramatic play of some hidden turmoil. "It's outmoded and in need of some minor repairs, I'm sure you won't care for the hassle of all that. Why don't I take you out to New Harbor, I'm sure that one will be far more to your liking. I can even take you by Emery house, I would hate for you to settle on something smaller and then decide after all you could use a spare room for guests…"

"Minor repairs, but nothing major?" Adele sank her thoughts into the statement which addressed her concerns, ignoring the rest. "Coral Cottage sounds quite reasonable, and I'm not opposed to a bit of cleaning and repair." Internally, she shuddered, but if it meant gaining her independence, she was willing to uncover whatever hidden strength she might possess. Her eyes wandered back to the barometer as she thought. The instrument seemed to gleam now, though she could ascertain no source of light which might cause the effect.

"Truly, ma'am, it would be a waste of your time to—"

She snapped her attention back to Mr. Alderman. "You said the kitchen was outmoded, but is it functional?"

"Well, yes, but—"

"I should like to see it."

"The kitchen?"

"The home."

"Oh," his shoulders slumped. "Truly, I'm sure it's not a good fit for you."

"I'd like to be the judge of that myself."

"Perhaps if you don't care for Emery house or New Harbor—"

Adele stood, drawing herself up to the extent of her small frame and jutting out her chin. "I believe I saw there were two realty offices in town," she hoped her guess based on newspaper adverts proved correct. "If you are disinclined to show me the place I'm curious about, perhaps the other office has Coral Cottage on their books as well." She began to turn her back on the realtor, moving as swiftly as she dared in her traitorous garb.

"I'd be quite happy to take you, ma'am," Mr. Alderman's pained voice rang out behind her as she reached the center of the office. Turning, she noted he looked anything but pleased about the state of affairs. His rounded eyes bobbed with an unspoken plea of reconsideration. "We can start with New Harbor—"

"I wish to begin with Coral Cottage, it sounds the most suited to my needs."

The Adam's apple at the center of his thin neck dipped dramatically before swinging violently toward his chin. A moment of silent battle ensued between his imploring eyes and her determination, ending when his chin drooped toward his chest. "Very well, as you like. I'll bring my car around."

Her eyes followed him as he maneuvered around the desk to precede her to the office door, wavering only once in their sentinel duty as he passed by the clock and barometer. The barometer practically shimmered now.

What on earth would cause such a play of light? The hues danced so gaily across the brass she could almost swear it was some inanimate form of a chuckle.

"Ma'am?" Mr. Alderman stood at the door, holding it open for her, pale as death as he followed her gaze to the barometer.

"What a peculiar piece," she noted, turning to join him with a shake of her head. Lovely, but peculiar."

CHAPTER 2

*oral Cottage resided in a sleepy cove town on the opposite side of Boston to that where Adele's mother-in-law lived, a fact which instantly endeared it to her. Somewhat out of the way, one had to embark on a steep and winding climb up a road called Mariner's Lane to reach it. The cliff outcroppings marking the end of the lane gave Adele's motherly heart a moment of angst, but the majority of the road, though steep, connected to far more gradual descents to the shore below.

She breathed in as deeply as she dared at the window, still shrouded in her veil. The air, crisp and salted, smoothed the frazzled edges of her nerves and set her at ease. At least until they rounded the final curve of the lane and her calm swiftly gave way to excitement.

The house loomed majestic above the bay, its position

above the rest of the town giving it the air of a sentinel lighthouse monitoring the sea rather than a family home. Even so, something in the proud building thrilled Adele and called to her the moment she spied it. It offered a distinct sense of sturdiness against the elements and protection from the world.

As they neared, Adele observed the dullness of the paint, a few leaning shutters, and a front garden sprawling jungle-like before the home. But from the foundation stones beneath the porch to the railing of the widow's walk, she could detect no indication of any major flaw in construction. Not that she knew much about architecture aside from a few words her late husband was wont to include in general conversation, but she felt any truly problematic inadequacies would make themselves known more easily to the viewer. She hoped.

"How is the roof?" She asked.

"What?" Mr. Alderman kept his gaze steadied on the home in front of them, the lines of his shoulders and back compressing and tightening as they neared.

"The roof. Is it watertight?"

"Oh, yes, the roof is perfectly serviceable." He pulled up to the front gate set between rough stone walls more suitable to an Irish field than a New England cottage, and turned off the motor. "Are you sure you won't reconsider viewing New Harbor first?"

"That would make no sense, Mr. Alderman. We're already here. I quite like the place, it's truly stunning in its craftsmanship." That much was true and required no architectural background to deduce. The home boasted enough commonplace features to blend in nicely with the town proper, though its position just on the outskirts of the community allowed it some room for experimentation, which the designer took full advantage of.

A balcony overlooking the sea jutted out from French doors on the second floor, a rounded turret graced the cliff-most side of the house, complete with weathervane. Several windows sported stained glass, and the molding framing the porch and eaves boasted delicate carving. Every detail seemed thought out with care. "Who designed the home?" She asked, impatience growing as her guide still made no move to exit the car.

"The original owner," he responded, still staring pointedly forward, hands gripping the steering wheel.

She pulled on the handle of her door, the resultant click of the latch prompting the man into motion. He scurried out and around to offer her his hand. She would have taken it in any case out of politeness, but an added benefit to his presence was that he blocked some of the wind which still threatened to take her by the hem and cast her into the sea. He also provided the service of aiding to hold down her veil as they made their way up the walk to the front door, beautifully carved and solid enough to withstand centuries of beating from gales.

"I thought you said the owner was a sea captain?" She

asked on a gasp once they entered the front entryway, sealing them off from the bluster of the world outside.

"He was." Offering no further explanation, the realtor moved toward a doorway opposite the front stairs. The size of the portal and tell-tale pocket doors indicated they were entering the sitting room, a fact confirmed a moment later when she stepped across the threshold.

An odd assortment of furniture met them, some of it covered over with sheets to keep the dust at bay. A dark-lacquered Chinese cabinet, whose doors depicted images of cranes and bamboo, sat beside what looked like an Amish-crafted hutch displaying a distinctly English silver tea set.

"The captain must certainly have been a bachelor to have maintained this hodgepodge collection of furnishings." She mused, running a gloved finger through the layer of dust obscuring the carved detail of a tray table. An odd sort of prickling took up at the base of her skull and down along her back, as though someone were staring at her or had run a finger along her back. She shifted her shoulders against a sudden shiver, turning her attention to the fireplace and a portrait above the mantle. "Who is that?"

The portrait was far from flattering, or even good in terms of skill, but something in the image drew her.

"That's the original owner of the home, Captain Gregory Daniels."

She stepped closer, taking in the positioning of the

subject, stiff and angular without dimension. He wore the typical uniform coat of a captain, along with the signature hat. One box-like hand clutched a cylinder she could only guess was meant to be a spyglass. Insignificant features, including a sharp nose and chin, were framed by wiry hair and beard in a yellow-orange color which failed completely in its attempt to imitate a natural hue.

Yet, oddly, the artist managed to convey an unnervingly lifelike quality to the eyes. Crystalline blue almost sparkling with... laughter? Furrowing her brow, she leaned in closer, only to straighten again an instant later. Some play of light in that moment almost convinced her the portrait had winked.

"Would you like to see the kitchen?" Mr. Alderman squeaked from behind her, distracting her. She turned in his direction.

"Oh, yes, thank you." She followed him out of the room, casting a parting glance over her shoulder at the portrait, whose eyes now stared as dull and lifeless as the rest of the piece.

"I understand now why you didn't want me to come here, Mr. Alderman," she began as they crossed the hall.

"You do?" He whirled about, eyes ready to burst through the confining glasses.

"It needs a good cleaning. How is it you haven't put the place in better order? No wonder it hasn't been rented yet. It must be years since this house was lived in. Or cleaned."

Another cloud of disappointment tinged with annoyance flitted across the man's countenance. "It has. Fifteen years in fact."

"How is it that the house came to be in such a forlorn state? You told me along the drive the captain had died, but had he no family to claim his things?"

"The captain's next of kin lives in South America and had no desire to sort through the property, only wished to have it rented."

"I see."

They moved through the formal dining room, every bit as shrouded and dust-laden as the sitting room, though Adele noted the space seemed just the right size to accommodate her small family with as much grace as a larger gathering. That earned the room a small nod of approval. The kitchen proved spacious enough without leaning toward pretentiousness. A well-lit space designed with efficiency in mind, even if the appliances were a bit dated. From the description in the catalog Adele worried she might find nothing but an over-sized hearth for cooking and a water pump in the yard. This kitchen was outfitted with a full faucet and sink, and a gas range. Perfectly suitable. She turned toward a small breakfast nook in the corner and paused.

"I thought you said the house hasn't been lived in?" She questioned.

The agent followed her gaze to where a plate of half-eaten food sat on the table beside an open newspaper and a near-empty cup of coffee. "Well, a cleaning woman came in last week."

Adele's eyes widened, taking in again the layer of dust lining every flat surface. "I hope you didn't pay her for her time!"

"As a matter of fact, no, she didn't stay the day and only got so far in her task as the front stairwell."

"But why—"

"Mrs. Monroe, I'm sure you can see this house is completely unsuitable for your needs, it would take far too much effort for you to put to rights. Why don't you let me drive you over to New Harbor?"

"I see no such thing, and we can't leave yet, we haven't seen the upstairs."

"It's really not—"

"I insist on seeing the upstairs. I'll take a full tour before making any decision." Without waiting for a response, she turned on her heel and darted toward the doorway, intent on reaching the stairs and making good on her threat.

~

THE FRONT STAIRCASE incorporated every aspect of formality one might expect of an upper-class home. Carved and polished banisters guided a guest up a set of carpeted stairs to a landing which displayed a garden scene of stained glass before changing direction sharply to continue the climb to the second floor. The angle necessitated a complete about-face for the person mounting the stairs and as Adele completed the movement she paused to gaze in wonder at this new view of the front entry.

Accumulated dirt on the window muted the effect, but what daylight shone through hinted at potential for a grand kaleidoscopic display when the sun shone fully through the colored glass and danced across both floor and chandelier. Indeed, the prismatic crystals of the chandelier would only heighten the effect. For a moment she imagined the front entry alive with brilliant color as guests arrived for an evening gathering and gasped in awe.

Her first reaction was to wonder yet again at the captain's foresight. She found it difficult to imagine any man, let alone a sea captain, dreaming up such wondrous details. She shook her head. More likely the effect of the window never occurred to him and was just a happy accident.

"Ha!" The rebuke sounded through her thoughts, causing Adele to start and look about.

"Something wrong, Mrs. Monroe?" Mr. Alderman asked from the base of the stairs. He awaited her response with something akin to eagerness.

"I thought I heard..." goodness, she must be letting the dreariness of the house's state get to her. Somewhere amid the rooms and halls a gust of wind must have found a sounding board in a crack or flue.

"Yes?" The realtor prompted.

"Nothing, just the wind." Continuing up the stairs, she came to a hallway with two doors on one side and one on the other. At the end of the hall yet another curious window drew her attention. She couldn't say she'd ever seen one quite like it. Round rather than rectangular, it carried itself more like a porthole than a proper window.

"The master bedroom is on the left here," Mr. Alderman chimed from behind her before she had the chance to inspect the window or its view more closely. "The doors on the right are the additional rooms."

Nodding, she allowed the man to lead her into the main bedroom. The space proved large and commanding, a strong contrast to the modest sizing of the main rooms. Yet, the room maintained the warmth and coziness of the rest of the house. There was space enough for a massive four-poster bed, though it looked as though a reasonably sized bed had been incorporated into the paneling at one side of the room, built-in on two sides, as one might expect to find on a ship. A cozy sitting area comprised of a wing chair and ottoman, plus a side table lounged in front of a gas fireplace, while a davenport desk took up space beside a row of bookshelves on the opposite wall. The focal point of the room, however, was an adornment set in front of the French doors Adele noticed on her initial observation of the house.

"A telescope?" She murmured.

"Unusual, to be sure," Mr. Alderman confirmed. "But lends a bit of character, I'd say."

"It certainly does." She approached the piece, again noting that strange prickling at the back of her neck. Ignoring the feeling, she focused on the telescope. Something seemed odd about it. She reached one small, gloved hand toward it, entranced by the sparkle of polished brass in what sunlight managed to filter through the grimy window.

"Polished!" She stated triumphantly.

"What?"

"This telescope, it's polished! I thought there was something odd about it. It's got to be the only clean thing in the entire house."

"Well, I suppose—"

The realtor's words drowned in the distinct rumble of a laugh. Not the creak of floorboards, not the wind in a flue, the rich baritone of a man's voice rolling through the air, along her spine, and tickling the side of her neck until she gasped.

"That's enough of a tour!" Mr. Alderman declared with more conviction than he'd heretofore mustered in any of his statements. "Mrs. Monroe, I insist we leave."

An electrified fluttering took up in Adele's chest, robbing her of breath. The continued echo of that mesmerizing voice seemed to sound from directly inside her mind, bypassing the efforts of her ears. These experiences so shocked her, she didn't note the press of Mr. Alderman's hand on her elbow until they reached the car. Mr. Alderman all but shoved her into the passenger seat and proceeded to race the conveyance pell-mell down the road toward town.

"Stop the car!"

The realtor ignored her.

"Mr. Alderman, I insist you stop this vehicle this instant!"

As though only just realizing his manic state and the potential danger of his erratic driving, Mr. Alderman slowed the car and came to a stop at the next turn-out. "My apologies, Mrs. Monroe. I just— well, now you see why I was so adamant about the house being unsuitable."

"I see why you didn't want me to visit the place, I fail to see how it is unsuitable."

"Fail to see? But it's obviously— It's—"

"Haunted?"

"Yes!"

"Come now, this is the twentieth century after all, how can you be so superstitious? Old houses make noise. Creaking floorboards, clanking pipes—"

"Did that sound like clanking pipes to you?" he stared at her agape.

"No," she admitted.

"It's an unsavory place, Mrs. Monroe, certainly no

place for a lady and her children. I cannot in good conscience allow you to stay there."

Adele pressed her lips together, shifting in her seat to stare out the back window, though Coral Cottage was no longer visible past the bend in the road. "Couldn't something be done to... exorcise the captain? I assume it is the captain who haunts the place." Why she assumed so mystified her, such a compelling voice reverberating through her every fiber and making her weak at the knees certainly didn't fit the caricature displayed in the former owner's portrait.

"Believe me, ma'am, I have attempted everything I could think of from calling in the nearest priest to conducting seances. None of it worked and no one who steps foot in that house stays longer than a day. It's hopeless."

"But why do you suppose the captain haunts it?"

"Your guess is as good as mine, but they say those who kill themselves are always restless spirits."

Adele gasped, eyes widening as she craned her neck toward the rear window again. "He killed himself?"

"I'm afraid so. Now, Mrs. Monroe, I'm sorry for this upsetting trip, I am more than happy to take you straight back to Newton. I can't imagine You have any desire to view additional homes today."

Facing forward in her seat, Adele chewed on her lip. A reckless thought formed in her mind, refusing to listen to reason. "Mr. Alderman, could you allow me to stay a night in Coral Cottage?"

"Are you mad?" The man swiveled in his seat to stare at her as though she'd sprouted a second head. "What on earth for?"

"I like the place and am of a mind to rent it."

"Forgive me, but haven't you heard anything I just said?"

"I've heard every word. For myself, I'm not concerned with ghosts. Who knows what the true source of the sound was, but if everyone who visits leaves at the slightest sound, no wonder the place has a negative reputation. Allow me one night. That will prove I have the wherewithal to remain in the home before you go through the trouble of preparing paperwork, and also allow me to ascertain if there is anything in the house which might frighten my children before I agree to rent it."

Mr. Alderman hesitated in his argument, but a moment later his business sense proved incapable of outweighing his conscience. "I'm sorry, Mrs. Monroe, but I simply cannot allow you to remain alone in that house."

"I could bring my housekeeper," she insisted. "A sturdier soul you'll never meet, why she could spar with the devil himself and come out the victor. You would have no reason at all to fear for our safety." She held her breath, watching intently as Mr. Alderman waged his internal battle.

He pressed his lips together with such force the surrounding skin whitened, staring out the windshield with intensity as his grip tightened on the steering wheel. "I'll have to wire the owner for his approval."

"That's no problem at all, it will give me time to make arrangements with my housekeeper. When would you expect a response?"

"Within two days I imagine."

"Perfect, then I shall come in three days. You'll see, Mr. Alderman, it will be beneficial to us both."

His expression indicated he held no such hope, but he said nothing as he restarted the car's engine and maneuvered back onto the road at a much more subdued speed than they'd previously traveled.

Excitement flooded Adele. To have her own living space and the independence that came with it! She would gladly contend with a ghost for that. She only hoped nothing would occur during her stay to force her to renege on the opportunity.

CHAPTER 3

Adele and Bessie arrived at Coral Cottage early on their appointed day, having received the approval from Mr. Alderman to stay at the house. Not for the first time she wondered at her mental state, given an utter lack of concern for the strange episode from the previous visit. She'd initially been startled and a bit frightened, despite her arguments to Mr. Alderman, but those feelings faded in the interim until she almost believed her arguments herself. A haunted house, what a preposterous idea. Even had any doubts lingered, Bessie was the best insurance to have against such ideas.

"This place is a right bit of work," the housekeeper clucked upon entering the kitchen with a shake of her head. "Well, best get on with it." Rolling up her sleeves and snatching an apron from the basket she carried, she made her way to the faucet with a bucket while Adele found a space to set out the foodstuffs they'd brought with for the stay.

"Well, now, that's rotten luck," the woman declared a few minutes later. Adele paused in the dusting she'd begun at the window of the breakfast nook to look over at her.

"What's wrong?"

The bucket of water sat atop one of the burners on the range and Bessie stood doubled over with her nose all but touching the edge of the appliance. "There's no gas. Did Mr. Alderman mention any troubles with the appliances?"

"No, none."

"Well, that's going to be a bother. We can't clean the place properly without hot water."

"I'll call Mr. Alderman and see what he suggests."

A short while later the women had moved on to some initial dusting, sweeping, and removing of dust sheets from furniture when a knock sounded at the back door. A young man, or rather a boy looking slightly older in experience than his years, stood outside with a small cast iron Golden Star stove in tow.

"Morning, ma'am," he nodded. "I'm from the general store. Mr. Hartford said you ordered up a sad iron?"

"That's right," Bessie confirmed. "You can set it over there." She waved at a general corner of the kitchen.

"All right," she clapped and rubbed her hands

together after the boy left again. "Now we can get to work."

With marked efficiency, Bessie set her wash water to boiling and the true cleaning began. Adele could honestly say she'd never worked so hard in her life, but despite the draining exertion of it and the knowledge she might not be able to drag herself from her bed in the morning, an unfounded giddiness infused in her. With each window that winked out of its slumber, every new surface revealed like a jewel of hidden treasure, she felt an ever-deepening belonging and satisfaction. By the time she and Bessie paused in their work to eat lunch, she already felt as though this were her home.

"We'd best do up the beds next," Bessie suggested around a bite of sandwich. "If we wait until the end of the day, we won't want to anymore and will have to sleep on the dust."

Adele smiled. "That would be a terrible waste of our efforts." She sipped at the cup of coffee in her hands, holding the cup between both her hands as was her habit, though spending the majority of the day dipping those hands into hot water negated any need for additional warmth at present. She might have liked to give in to her fatigue and linger over lunch, but Bessie, stalwart housekeeper that she was, allowed for no entertaining of such thoughts.

"Come on, then, Miss," she insisted as she cleared

away the dishes. "This ship isn't going to get *itself* seaworthy."

"Why, Bessie, there's some parlance I can't say I've heard you use before."

Bessie paused, thinking over her words. "You're right. I suppose it's the salty air addling my mind. Can't say I'm used to air this fresh. Might not be good for the constitution."

The women made their way upstairs, Adele happy to see she wasn't the only one moving slowly, though the thought occurred to her Bessie might not want to let her feel weak and so feigned fatigue herself. For all her saltiness, the woman cared dearly for her mistress and Adele knew it.

"What an odd arrangement for a bedroom," Bessie shook her head on entering the master bedroom and seeing the sparse and odd collection of furnishings. "You'd think the man would have taken more care to provide himself a bit of comfort after a life at sea. Especially with the time he took mapping out the rest of the place."

"Perhaps he'd grown so far accustomed to things this way it didn't occur to him," Adele shrugged, stripping the dusty, half moth-eaten bedding from the bed. Bessie reached for the pillow, masterfully recovering it in the fine soft linen Adele had brought before beginning to unfold the larger bedsheets. "Or perhaps he never got around to it. I gather from Mr. Alderman the captain hadn't been in residence long when he passed."

"There's a shame. He took ill?"

"Suicide."

Bessie paused in her work, dragging one corner of the bed sheet up to her hip along with the fist she set there. "Well, if that isn't a foolish way to go. I wouldn't have taken a sea captain for such a coward."

A gust of wind caught the window left open earlier in the day to help air the house and sent it slamming against the wall. Adele rushed over to close it, yelping when she caught her finger in the latch. "Oh, bother!" Shaking her hand and head, she returned to Bessie. Between the two of them, they made quick work dusting and sweeping, then moved on to one of the smaller rooms, which would house Bessie for the night.

By the time they finished their evening repast, though barely nine o'clock, both of them could hardly keep from yawning their exhaustion.

"You'd best take yourself to bed, Bessie. I'll put up the dishes and do the same in a moment."

"I'll get the dishes, Miss, you needn't bother with it."

"It won't take but a moment, I insist." She all but shoved Bessie toward the doorway, not that the woman would have moved if she'd truly been unwilling to give over the task. She had the permanence of a brick wall when she so desired. With a nod and a half-swallowed thank you as another yawn beset her, she wandered upstairs.

Adele filled the wash bucket part way with water and set it atop the sad iron they'd been using, only to find to her chagrin as she attempted to light it, they'd depleted the oil.

"Oh, bother," she grumbled, staring daggers at the bucket with hands on hips before narrowing her eyes at the gas range. "Mr. Alderman said there was no reason you shouldn't work," she accused. They'd ordered the tank based on the fact they would only be a day, which wasn't likely enough time for Mr. Alderman to have the problem looked at and repaired.

Crossing her arms under her chest, she tilted her head toward the appliance and pursed her lips. With a determined huff, she hauled the bucket from its place and set it atop the stove. Turning the knob for the burner, she listened. Nothing. She flicked it off and turned again. Nothing.

"For heaven's sake," she slapped her palms against her thighs. "Why won't you work?"

"Because I don't wish it to work."

Adele spun around, eyes wide, only to gaze into an empty room. Heart racing, she swallowed. Had she truly heard something? Of course she had. And to her chagrin it sounded a great deal like the tones of that rumbling laughter she so recently convinced herself she *hadn't* heard. But how? There was obviously no one in the room.

"I don't care for gas," the voice returned, and she realized it had the same uncanny quality to it she'd noted previously, as though it emitted directly from her thoughts rather than go through the interpretation of her ears.

"Didn't want the damned stuff in the first place, but the confounded workman convinced me it was best. Modernization. Bah!"

"Captain Daniels?" Adele blinked, eyes still wandering from floor to ceiling in their attempt to attach something tangible to the voice in her head.

"None other. I can't say it's a pleasure, Madam. Why are you in my home?"

"I mean to live here."

"Do you? Don't know where you got the notion I'd allow it. You may stay the night, as I never was the sort to cast a woman out from shelter into the night, even a trespassing vagrant, but I expect you and your accomplice to shove off in the morning."

Adele stiffened her spine, anger dimming her good sense and muting the oddity of the situation. "How dare you. I am a prospective tenant to this home, here with the permission of the owner."

"That blasted wharf-rat in South America is not the owner of this house!" The captain roared through her mind. "Bad enough some scoundrel lawyer had the audacity to name him my next of kin! I won't have renters in my home. Especially not a woman. I meant this home to act as a retirement home for seamen."

"Then why didn't you arrange it that way before you killed yourself?"

"Because I did not kill myself! I fell asleep in front of the damned gas fireplace in my room. Must have kicked the damned valve with my foot in my sleep."

"Must you use such language?"

"There's nothing wrong with my damned language!"

Rolling her eyes, Adele continued. "Mr. Alderman said your cleaning woman attested that your windows were closed, but she'd never known you to close them, day or night."

"And no one questioned how she knew that! I never invited her to sleep with me! There was a storm blowing the rain in through the window and ruining my floors and curtains. I shut the window. Do you mean to tell me you'd have done any differently?"

"No, I wouldn't have."

"There."

"But the fact remains, you died without leaving provisions for the house, it is now owned by a relation of yours, and I mean to live here." Forgetting the dishes and the water, she spun on her heel and made her way up to the bedroom.

"Absurd," Adele muttered to herself as she turned down the freshly made bed. The realization she'd been standing in the kitchen arguing with a voice in her head had caused her abrupt departure from the kitchen. She must be extremely tired. Either that or she was going mad. Having rolled down her sleeves from her elbows, she reached for the buttons of her blouse at her neck.

"There is nothing absurd about my defense of my home." Captain Daniels' voice insisted, sending her heart shooting up into her throat. "Neither are you going mad. Now, why do you wish to live here?"

Peering into the darkened corners of the room, Adele fought her frantic pulse. "I have no desire to argue with you, Captain, I wish to prepare for bed, now please leave."

"Prepare all you like, but without confirmation you intend to leave this house in the morning and not return, make no mistake you will have an argument on your hands."

"I can't prepare for bed with you here, please leave."

"Why the devil not? Confound it woman, I've been dead nearly two decades. My flesh and any earthly desires that went along with it are void. A better tactic, should you wish for me to leave, is to answer the question I've posed."

"You wouldn't understand my sentiment, you've obviously too hard a heart. I shall take up my inquiry with Mr.

Alderman in the morning and there will be nothing you can do about it."

"Oh no? Upon my word, though I pride myself no woman has ever been the worse for knowing me, on the matter of my property I am not above creating a living hell to dissuade you."

Adele remembered why she requested this stay in the first place. She might be willing to suffer an irate ghost on the grounds of reasonable rent, but she couldn't stand for anything to frighten her children. "The house needs me."

"The house needs nothing of the sort."

"It does. With no one here to care for it, it will fall into even greater disrepair. How is that a testament to what you'd planned for it?"

"I would rather it fall into disrepair than be rented out to blasted tenants who would actively tear it to bits."

"I wouldn't do that. I want a home, someplace warm and sturdy to raise my children. If you care so much for this house, you ought to consider what's best for the house. Didn't you mean for it to be warm and inviting if you envisioned a rest home?"

A long pause ensued.

"Couldn't you allow me to stay here on trial? Six months? I could prove what good care I'd take of the place."

"Give a man an inch, he'll take a mile. Women are worse. Even so, there might be a measure of reason in your request. Very well, you may stay through the spring."

"Oh, wonderful! And you'll leave and not bother us that whole time?"

"Of course not, blast it! This is my home."

Her shoulders sagged. She spent some time deep in thought trying to find a solution. In the end she shook her head. "Well, after all that you'll have your way after all. I can't bring my children here."

"Why not?"

"How in the world would I explain you to them? And aside from that, you'd be a terrible influence with your language and questionable sailor's morals."

"Seaman, blast it! Sailor is a landlubber's word. My language is damned impeccable, and so are my morals. Your brats will not be ill-influenced by me."

"Even so, Children are wont to tell tales, it won't do any of us any good to start telling tales of ghosts. No, it was kind of you to relent and allow us to stay, but I'll have to abandon the idea. A shame, I do feel as though this house was practically calling to me to restore some life to it."

Tears stung at Adele's eyes, and she sniffed. Exhaustion no doubt amplified her disappointment, but the words rang true. In the span of only a few hours she'd come to consider the place her home. Her lip trembled.

"Here, now, belay that! I cannot abide a woman's crying."

"I'm sorry, Captain, but I can't help it. The house seemed so appreciative of our efforts today, I was looking forward to making it shine."

"What a lot of drivel." The captain's voice faded away and Adele held her breath. Weariness weighed down on her and her eyelids drooped. Remembering the bed and the hour, she dabbed at her eyes with a handkerchief and proceeded to get herself changed and tucked into bed.

"I have it!" The captain's voice pounded through her thoughts just as she began to drift into sleep, sending her sitting up in a panic, clutching the blanket up to her chin. "What if I promise to restrict my wandering to my bedroom and the widow's walk? Your children would have practically no chance of encountering me in that arrangement."

"You haven't been here the entire time, have you?"

"That's neither here nor there. What do you say to my proposal?"

"It's very much here and there. Did you not even give me a moment's privacy?"

"Damn it, Madam, concentrate. Would the arrangement of my limited roaming be acceptable to you?"

"If you remain in this bedroom, where will I sleep?"

"In this bedroom."

"That's impossible!"

"Only to your feather-brained mind! I am quite losing patience with you."

With a growl, Adele slumped back down to the

mattress, rolling to face the wall and tugging the blanket up to her ears.

"Very well, then, I shall take up watch on the widow's walk for tonight. You might thank me in the morning for my consideration of your unfounded concerns."

Adele scrunched her eyes shut.

"By the way, you have a fine figure, you ought to be proud of it and not covering it up with all that black drab."

She rolled back to face the room, out of instinct she supposed as she knew by now no figure would greet her. But Captain Daniels was truly gone this time, she knew it in the stillness and dull quality of the emptiness around her.

CHAPTER 4

Sleep must have come swiftly, for Adele hardly noted closing her eyes before that weightless sensation known only in those moments when one is no longer tied to conscious thought settled around her. She dreamed as though she were awake, still in bed and observing the room about her. In her dream she thought she ought to worry over what was to become of her and her children. This fine home had been so close to theirs. But try as she might, no sense of worry overtook her. Instead, a deep warmth surrounded her, providing an unfelt embrace and all the calmness of deep security.

A movement on the far side of the room diverted her attention, a blur of color like a smudge of paint across canvas. A wisp of smoke, dark blue fading to white, slowly the form of another occupant in the room took shape. Even without seeing it fully, she knew it was

Captain Daniels. He paced near the telescope, first lumbering in one direction then the next in that rolling fashion taken on by men accustomed to adjusting balance on a rocking ship.

He wore his dark navy pea coat turned up at the collar, one hand tucked into a pocket, the other holding a pipe on which he gnawed absently. That hand looked nothing like the lifeless, wooden rendering of his portrait. That tanned hand was broad and firm, capable of holding a wheel against angry currents or commanding the securing ropes of rigging unwilling to be lashed down in a storm.

Turning his back on the darkness outside, he marched toward the fireplace, leaning in to inspect the bricks and gas valve with a deep frown. It struck Adele, as she watched him fold himself forward to his task, then straighten again, he was a much taller man than his portrait suggested. Tall and trim, broad shouldered and sturdy, he exuded the aura of a man who would have dared the elements to knock him down aboard his ship. Not at all the figure of a man who would have taken his own life. Had Adele harbored any doubts about his earlier explanation, they all vanished now.

Apparently satisfied in his inspection of the fireplace, he angled in her direction. Adele's heart thrilled, though the feeling proved difficult to place in the moment. She could have recognized it in an instant if she'd had any concept of her corporeal form, but at the moment she existed as a dimensionless sense of self within hazy surroundings. Therefore, she felt something akin to a shiver, if that feeling could be omnipresent in a space. His features, as they solidified before her, also bore little resemblance to their pale counterparts in the painting from the sitting room.

He came very near, pausing beside the bed and again leaning down to peer at her. Wavy hair and a neatly trimmed beard shone not quite golden but not dark either, more of a deep amber that one expected to adjust in depth according to the mood of his surroundings, glinting like a lion's mane in the sun or deepening to warm honey when moonlight reflected off the night sea. The angles of his jaw and nose cut sharp and precise away from his face, reminding Adele of sketches of old Nordic conquerors. And yet, something soft and languid lingered in his eyes of bright blue, an unexpected depth of kindness. He remained standing there only a brief while, but during those seconds Adele experienced an unerring sense of safety, a protective shield about her.

But then he retreated, moving back to the window and opening it before again taking up his pacing. He wore a concerned expression and fretted in his movements. To Adele it looked as though he were trying to sort through some distressing dilemma. So real did her dream feel to her that she didn't notice her transition from sleep to wakefulness until she shivered and noted the distinct sensation of muscles clenching and releasing in the process. The weightlessness vanished and she sank into the mattress of the bed. In the first moments of cognizance, her mind failed to make the connection with her body and her eyes instinctively looked toward the window in search of Captain Daniels, who must surely still be there.

Only darkness met her gaze, punctuated by a lone wash of silver moonlight painted across the floor. A flutter of white brought her attention back to the windows, one of which stood open, its light linen curtain fluttering against the cold breeze which had woken her. Mustering up control of her limbs, she sat up with a barely restrained groan and padded over to shut the window. Closing the latch sparked something in her memory.

"I closed you," she mumbled, staring at the latch. Too groggy to attempt making any further connection, she stepped to the side to take in the view from the French doors. A vast expanse of blue-black water glistened under the glow of a bright white moon, the sky a matte reflection extending the vision out into eternity. Suddenly aware of her small stature and limited life experience, she found herself wondering what lay beyond the horizon.

"A treasure trove of adventure and beauty," The captain's voice drifted into her thoughts as gently as fog settling upon the harbor. "You ought to explore it, you know."

"I have two children. My place is on land. It would

have been nice to dream though, with such a fine view to inspire me."

"Stay. I can provide the details to your imagination."

"How can I share a home with a ghost?"

"In the same manner you shared a home with a husband, I imagine."

"Impertinent."

"Truthful. It's not as though you loved the man."

That snapped Adele fully awake with an angry gasp.

"You needn't become defensive at the observation. You may have cared for the man, but you most certainly did not love him."

"And how would you know that?"

"Death has a way of providing clarity in all things. One soul bleeds into the next, human beings share memory and emotion far more than they are ever aware of. That's the root of empathy and feelings of having experienced something once already. Without the encumbrance of a mortal shell, one is free to drift through these memories and sensations."

"That seems very intrusive."

"I suppose it is to the limited thought of the earth-bound."

"Why did you open the window, you nearly froze me to death."

"Dramatics. You were in no threat of death. I opened the window because I didn't want yet another claim of suicide in my home."

"I assure you I mean to survive the night. Please keep the window closed for the duration of it."

Weariness and aching muscles again settling down on her, Adele turned back to the bed, crawling into its lingering warmth and curling up on her side. She knew her mind was only half aware, but she nursed an uncanny desire to return to that dream state. To the warmth and security of it. Within moments she felt herself drifting into the abyss again, cocooned in a sense of calm, breathing in the light fragrance of clean damp wool, sea salt, and sweet tobacco.

~

Morning shone bright through the window as Adele stretched in place under the covers. The stark contrast of light and silent emptiness against her swiftly fading memories of the night before almost served to convince Adele her interaction with the captain had all been a dream. Almost. Some invisible headiness lingered in the air like the pipe smoke she'd dreamed of. A vibrancy occupied this home in a way she'd never experienced in another. The house felt somehow more... alive than the materials of its construction warranted.

She wandered back through the haze of her dreams, recalling to mind the features of the man she'd envisioned pacing the room. Her cheeks burned. How could her imagination have concocted such an impossibly handsome man? Even if some stroke of subconscious brilliance mustered it, no explanation existed for their conversation. She never used foul language, even to herself. She couldn't have created such an experience from the desert of her imagination.

The scent of fresh coffee drifted upstairs to shake her from her pondering and entice her down for breakfast. Dressing as swiftly as her aching muscles would allow, she hurried downstairs. Bessie awaited her with a simple yet hearty meal which served well to put Adele at ease.

"Will you look at that, Miss," Bessie nodded toward the stove. "That range wouldn't light for nothing all day yesterday, and this morning it came right to life, easy as you please."

Adele gulped her coffee, flinching and staving off a bout of coughing when the still hot liquid scalded her throat. "How peculiar," she croaked, losing her appetite for the remainder of her breakfast.

She helped Bessie with the dishes and dove straight into reversing some of their work from the day before. The women stripped the bedding and refolded it, gathered up what cleaning supplies and remaining foodstuffs they'd brought with them, and generally made ready for the arrival of the car that would take them back to town.

"I think that's everything, Miss," Bessie announced as they set their belongings beside the door. "It's a fine day out, unseasonable warm. Would you like to sit out on the porch to wait?"

"I don't think so, Bessie, but you're welcome to if you like. I'd like to take a look at the harbor from the balcony upstairs. You know I think that's my favorite view from this house."

"Have you decided if you want to stay?"

She opened her mouth to let Bessie know she'd decided in the negative, but something caught the words in her throat so that all she could do was shake her head. "It's certainly a lovely space, isn't it? Or at least it will be with a bit more cleaning."

"I can't say it's unpleasant, no, and at least it doesn't need extensive work."

The prickling at the back of her neck started up again. Adele had completely forgotten the sensation. It drew her attention to the stairs. "Will you let me know when the car gets here, Bessie?"

"Yes, Miss."

Upstairs, the master bedroom welcomed her with the bright, childlike glee of late morning. The sun no longer shone directly through the windows but remained near enough to brighten both the room and her spirits. She stepped around the telescope to open the French doors, smiling the instant a cool breeze caressed her, the soft balancing touch to the sun's warm kiss. Breathing in deeply, she stood a moment with eyes closed and head tilted up to the sky.

Letting out a sigh, she brought her attention to the small harbor, stepping up to the railing and gazing out over the sparkling sea. A few specks in the distance made their way in one direction or another. She knew them to be fishing trawlers, but had to squint to make out their shapes, so near to the horizon. A memory flashed and she smiled with delight before rounding again toward the interior of the bedroom.

She'd never looked through a telescope, the childlike desire assaulted her on first seeing the item, but she hadn't the chance. Now she could. Grinning, she hurried behind the piece and tossed her veil behind her, taking hold of the instrument with gloved hands and peering through the eyepiece. All at once, those vague dots on the horizon took shape, boats of various colors and sizes, all wandering the waves on their particular mission.

"A transfixing sight, isn't it? The motions of man, made so small and insignificant against the backdrop of an endless sea." This time when the captain's voice rang through her thoughts, she accepted it as real without question. How quickly she seemed to flip between belief and disbelief. That knowledge somehow bothered her more than the idea of conversing with a ghost.

"It is, and I'm surprised at the viewing distance of this telescope. It's quite powerful."

"Of course it is, I spared no expense. A man of the sea does not easily resign himself to land, I wanted something that would take me as far out to sea as possible whenever I pleased."

"It's beautiful. But you know the components look a

great deal like those of a barometer in Mr. Alderman's office."

"They ought to," The Captain's voice turned steely. "I had both pieces commissioned together. That damned *kinsman* of mine gave Alderman the barometer to prevent him from quitting his contract after I ran off the third prospective renter."

"I'm sorry," Adele searched for a change of subject. "You know, for all my time living so near Boston, I've never been aboard a ship."

"You would have enjoyed it, I'm sure."

"What makes you so sure? I might be plagued with seasickness the moment I step foot on a ship."

"No, you've got a stronger constitution than that. You're stronger in general than the world takes you for, aren't you?"

She hesitated, uneasy at the depth of the captain's intrusion into her feelings. She'd long resented people's insistence that her small stature indicated fragility.

From her vantage point, she could see a fair distance down the road and noted a land-bound speck approaching. "Thank you for the vote of confidence, Captain. I wish you and the house well."

"You say that in a tone of parting."

"Yes, I told you I can't stay here."

"And I told you, you can. In fact, you will."

"Captain—"

"I've come up with the perfect solution, and mind this is my final offer."

"I didn't ask for an offer."

"Only because you haven't had the sense to. I've hit upon a solution which would at once fulfill both of our needs."

"Both of our needs?"

"Yes. You wish to stay here, and I have no wish to deal with renters. Therefore, you shall buy the house on the condition that you do as I originally intended and leave instruction in your will to convert the place to a retired seaman's home upon your death."

Adele nearly spun around, remembering in the final instant it would be fruitless to do so. "How in the world do you expect me to buy this house? Has it occurred to you that a woman willing to negotiate living in a haunted house might be doing so because it comes at a bargain price?"

"You will buy the house with my money. I had some hidden about the property and those vultures who laid claim to the place never knew of it."

"I can't do that, it's stealing."

"Good heaven's woman, do you not know the definition of that word? It's not stealing if I give it to you, now is it?"

"You're dead, by rights that money belongs to your kinsman."

"My kinsman be damned! Do you want to stay here or don't you?" The captain roared.

Adele bit her lip.

"That's better." His voice calmed. "Now listen to me, you will go into town today and advise Mr. Alderman that one night in this home has so thoroughly enchanted you that you wish to make an offer for the place."

"You call that a night of enchantment?" She lifted a brow.

"My apologies for lack of practice in recent years. Are you listening to what I'm telling you?"

"Yes, yes, I heard you. But what if that relative of yours doesn't accept the offer?"

"If he has any sense at all he'll accept."

"But what if he doesn't?"

A rumbling akin to faint thunder drifted through Adele's thoughts and if she had to hazard a guess, she assumed that was the ghostly equivalent to an angry sigh.

"I'm beginning to remember why I never allowed a woman aboard my ship. I may have wasted my effort in concocting this scheme. Perhaps I ought to reconsider."

"I'll make the offer," she rushed to confirm. "I just don't understand how you can be so sure it will work."

"I am sure because it is what I want and therefore it will come to pass. This is a basic law of existence. Luckily, I knew it already in life."

"I'm not surprised." Adele muttered.

"Miss?"

This time Adele did spin around to find Bessie standing in the doorway. "Yes?"

"The car is here, Miss."

Adele started. For a moment she'd completely forgotten the house didn't yet belong to her. "Oh, yes, of course." She moved to secure the French doors and followed Bessie out of the house, wondering if this scheme of the captain's truly would work.

CHAPTER 5

To her great surprise, the purchase of Coral Cottage transpired without issue. The house's owner proved all too willing to divest himself of the property for a paltry sum and none of Adele's family questioned her procurement of the funds to do so. That in itself appeared suspicious to her mind, but she could think of no explanation and honestly didn't care to. The house was hers and she looked forward to settling into her new life of independence.

Or so she thought. Within a few days of the move, she came to realize cohabitation with a ghost might test her patience almost as sorely as staying with her in-laws had.

"I TELL YOU, I'll be hanged if you move even one item from its place!" The captain bellowed through her thoughts as she navigated the parlor. She set down a vase on a side table, cocked her head to examine the configuration then, giving her head a small shake, removed the vase and returned it to the sideboard from whence she procured it.

The children were away at school and Bessie had gone into town to buy groceries, so the captain apparently felt no constraint to honor his promise to remain upstairs. The result proved both irritating and problematic for Adele.

"That's an empty threat and you know it," she grumbled, applying her dust rag to the windowsill. "You can't possibly be hanged. And I tell you again, you must be reasonable. This is my home now too, and I'll have it suit me. Haven't I already consented not to make changes to the bedroom? You might allow me some freedom of expression in the rest of the house, which I remind you, you promised not to disturb with your chain rattling and moaning."

"I do not moan."

"I've done my best to remove all that I can to the attic. If we put anything else up there the ceiling is liable to cave in."

"Which is why you should have left things as they were," he growled. "I collected those pieces of furniture and decor from the far corners of the world, they are all of highest quality and perfectly serviceable."

She nodded, taking up a small portrait and holding it

up to the wall, attempting to discern the most beneficial placement. "And the place looked exactly as though a bachelor had cobbled the decor together."

"What's that supposed to mean?"

"It means," she shook her head and set down the portrait, wandering across the room to remove the dust sheet from a side chair, "not one piece matched with any of the others. Some of them are truly lovely, but others..."

"Name one item which was not suitable for refined taste."

"That hideous tribal mask with the red eyes and fangs that looked prepared to pounce on anyone who came too close."

"That mask was a gift of honor given to me by the Chieftain himself for rescuing his daughter from the devious intent of a neighboring tribesman."

"It's hideous."

"Never count on a woman in matters of significance."

"It gave my poor little Henry nightmares his first night here."

"All they care for is that the drapes match the coloring of the carpet."

"Exactly, which is why that gaudy carpet had to go."

"The finest weaving from Persia!"

"The finest weaving by a blind craftsman, and moth-eaten to boot!"

The wind outside rattled the shutters. Not for the first time, Adele wished she had possession of the barometer from Mr. Alderman's office. The erratic weather in her new hometown seemed distinctly unnatural at times and she felt sure such an instrument might provide insight into the captain's moods. Not that they varied much. Grumpy, irritated, cantankerous, commanding, and petty were the most common. She doubted jovial ever made an appearance.

"If you made free to move practically all of my furniture into the attic," Captain Daniels argued, "which by the way, Madam, defeated the purpose of moving into a furnished house, why are you so intent now on discarding this hutch?"

She'd returned to the furniture item in question, the one which had started their argument. Earlier in the day, the owner of the local shop for second-hand and antique items arrived at her request. He'd inspected the piece, offered a price for it and, because she'd requested a day to think over the amount, promised to pick up the piece at her convenience. Knowing the captain's temperament, she'd actually requested the day in preparation of arguing her point, not to consider price.

"Because I have found no reasonable way to move it into the attic and have no reason to keep it." She stated.

"It will fit in the attic."

"It may fit, but there is no way to move it there. The stairs are too narrow and there is no good route to create a pulley system outside to lift it up to the only window that might admit it. That grotesque monkey-puzzle tree of yours bars the way." That tree was bound to be another argument, as she was keen on removing it, but it could wait for another day. "I'm sorry, Captain, but it must go. I've exhausted all other options."

"You have not."

"And which, pray tell, have I missed? Is there a hidden dumbwaiter to the attic large enough to house a massive and impossibly heavy hutch that I am unaware of?"

"Your sarcasm, Madam, does not aid your cause. You might simply ask my assistance."

Adele massaged her temples and turned her back on the hutch, perhaps seeking an escape through the doorway directly across from her. "As of my last contemplation of your form, I was quite sure you were without physical presence, in which case I fail to see how you might be of assistance."

"You've been contemplating my form, have you? I'm flattered. However, it seems you understand nothing of the unearthly realms. I would assist as I just did."

"What do you mean as you just— Where's the hutch?" She'd spun around, momentarily forgetting the fact the captain wouldn't be visible in the room. The hutch, commanding a substantial swathe of the room only moments before had vanished.

"In the attic." The captain's voice tickled her thoughts, distinctly chipper and boyish now that he'd got his way.

"How did you do that?" She breathed, stunned

curiosity outweighing the irritation at his having fun at her expense.

"The nature of the universe is far more fluid and malleable than mankind comprehends. The shift, in actuality, occurs in a similar fashion to how you moved the vase from one end of the room to the other a few moments ago. "

"But that's impossible!" she still gaped at the open space in front of her in disbelief. "It goes against the laws of nature."

"It goes against the laws of nature as mortal man understands them, which I daresay is a poor and disjointed understanding at best."

"But..."

A sound akin to a sigh rustled through Adele's mind a moment before the captain's response issued, his words taking on the rare gentle tone she often craved in their moments of angry discussion. "Suffice it to say, my dear, that could nature, in her sublime and enlightened beauty, speak directly to man, she would attest to daily wonders the likes of which man has not actively witnessed since biblical times."

"I've often wished to see such things," she mused. "To believe in a world much more magical than the one we drift through so dully." Her cheeks heated. What had brought those thoughts into being? True, in her childhood and early youth she fantasized often of mythical creatures and fairy tale magic, but such fancies were foolish and outside the realm of adult responsibility.

"You can, my dear," the captain's rich, velvety baritone caressed her heart, sending it into flutters, "And it is..." his voice trailed away like a lazy summer breeze, dousing her in warmth serene enough to make her sigh.

The front door creaked, signaling Bessie's return.

"Wouldn't you know, I found more than I was looking for, but the boy from the grocers was able to cart me back up here." The housekeeper reported. "He'll help bring the bags in, can I bother you to start the cook pot boiling, Miss?"

Adele snapped out of her reverie and all but ran for the kitchen. "Yes, of course."

∽

A LOW FIRE glowed and crackled in the hearth. Not quite spring yet, but the days shone consistently warmer with intermittent showers. Along the roadway edges and in the gardens, crocuses, daffodils, tulips and snowdrops denied any late-season snowfall. Adele leaned her head against the wing of her armchair and stretched her toes a hint closer to the fire.

In her hand rested the latest news from her mother-in-law. The woman's letters resembled poorly disguised novels in which she felt compelled to report in fine detail all news and gossip pertaining to anyone in her immediate sphere of influence. Thus, Adele often put off reading the happily infrequent missives until evening after the children had gone to bed. Even then the process often required multiple sittings.

"You're prowling, I can tell by the uneasy waves in my fire flames," she noted, eyes still steadied on her letter, though she hardly took note of the words. It wasn't really the fire that alerted her to the captain's presence, but a headiness in the room, a warm weight to the very air which signaled companionship. She'd become so perceptive of it, and developed a distinct preference for it, that she no longer fussed if the captain chatted with her if she were alone somewhere downstairs.

"Is that blasted fire really all that necessary?" He grumbled, forcing Adele to smother a smile. Their initial arguments over particulars of the house having eased as they each became accustomed to the new arrangement, his sourness now produced more amusement than annoyance.

"The depth of winter may be behind us, but the night temperatures are still freezing." She asserted. "And don't you dare open the window while I'm sleeping again, that's a terrible habit of yours. My lips were blue when I got up the other day. I know little inconveniences like temperature don't affect you anymore, but you should at least remember that we mortals require a certain amount of warmth to survive."

A faint rumbling emitted from somewhere far out to

sea. Another squall approaching? Or just the captain grumbling? These things were still so difficult to differentiate. She set down her letter, admitting defeat and rubbing at her eyes.

"More banalities from your mother-in-law I take it?" Captain Daniels asked, the rumbling over the ocean fading into night. "You never look so weary as after reading one of her letters. Why do you bother?"

"She often makes commentary regarding the children and on occasion there might be information she expects them to know. If they fail to recite properly to her questions when they visit, I'll have weeks' worth of complaints to deal with. I view these letters as the lesser evil."

"So, what is she harping about now?"

"More of the same, she's concerned about the children and I living in isolation." Hefting herself up from the chair, Adele made her way to the French doors to pull the curtains shut. A brief glimmer of light on the horizon indicated a storm somewhere just out of sight.

"You're not on the damned Arctic tundra! This is a perfectly acceptable town. Large enough to provide the basic amenities, small enough to avoid mingling with the masses if you so choose, that's why I chose the place for my final port."

"I agree with you, but I'm afraid my in-laws are incapable of seeing it that way."

"Well then your in-laws can take a long walk off a short—"

"Please be civil, Captain! After all, they are my family. I think she'd be more amiable if I remarried, though that goes against her ideas of my proper behavior as a widow, so she only skirts around the topic."

Stillness settled in the air, a quiet of that ominous sort which could herald either the onset of a cyclone or its end with equal conviction.

"You're not going to argue that point?" She hazarded, wondering at the captain's sudden dearth of commentary.

"No, I think she's quite right. A woman ought to have a man about the place." He made the statement with certainty, though his tone smacked of vexation.

"Now you're showing your age, Captain. It's the twentieth century, you know. Women are perfectly capable of living independent lives and making informed decisions. I hear we're getting close to winning the vote."

"Bah! Women have been arguing for the vote for decades, if not centuries!"

"Yes, and our perseverance may finally see success soon."

"Now that you've sufficiently worn down the collective will of generations of men?"

This particular theme held too much potential for argument for Adele to enjoy at the moment. She much preferred pleasant haunting. "Whatever your opinions on the necessity of a woman aligning herself with a man, I didn't note any particular advantage in my situation while married."

A HAUNTING LOVE

"Because you married the wrong man."

She paused in removing her robe to drape across the foot of the bed. When had she lost her concern about impropriety? "Don't start that again. Are you going to argue I ought to remarry? I can't imagine that going well for our particular living arrangement."

"You're right, it wouldn't. And no, I will not encourage you to remarry. There is already a man about the place, you simply have the unfortunate circumstance of being unable to mention it."

She slipped under the covers, propping herself up against the pillows.

"What's got you restless, my dear? You appear far more awake now than you were in the chair. Have I disturbed you with my opinions?"

"No, I was just thinking of the early days of my marriage. It was a grand time of lofty dreams."

"What did he promise you, dear?" the captain's voice soothed, encouraging her eyelids to droop once more.

"Before we married, my husband often spoke about taking me to Europe or out west. I liked the idea of seeing the world. It was always what we would do once his firm became more established. But it was never quite established enough. Then the children came, and he promised when they were a bit older..."

"Europe wouldn't have been grand enough for you, my dear. You are better suited to the more exotic."

She scooted further beneath the covers and snuggled

65

her cheek into her pillow like a child. "I doubt that, but thank you. Tell me about the places you've been. What were they like?"

The captain made no objection, regaling her with tales of beauty and excitement recited in tones so soft she didn't notice the transition from waking into sleep. In her dreams she sailed alongside him into far-reaching ports as he smiled handsomely and pointed out the best each had to offer.

An Asian city glowed with the soft light of countless paper lanterns. Somewhere near the silk road between India and Persia the ship became a floating perfumery, laden with sumptuous spices and fragrant oils. The sky came alive with color amid the icy northern fjords. Had any wandering angels paused to observe her that night, they could not have missed the serene smile adorning her features.

CHAPTER 6

*S*pring faded almost as swiftly as it arrived, giving way to warm days, busy docks, and Adele's children clamoring for both the end of school and days spent wandering the shore in search of pirate treasure. Yet Adele took little note of the season awaited by so many. Indeed, as the temperature rose, so did her nervousness. She hid the fact well enough from her children, and Bessie may suspect but knew better than to ask, but one resident of Coral Cottage would not be put off.

"You've been unduly preoccupied by the newspaper of late. What has you so enthralled?" The captain stole into her thoughts the instant Bessie marched upstairs to begin her cleaning tasks.

Adele allowed her hands to fall onto the dining table in front of her, crumpling the *Cove Gazette* she held in the process. "Must you interrupt my breakfast?"

"Your breakfast has been cold for the better part of the last hour and there's more chance of the mouse in the wall stealing it from under your nose than of you eating it."

"There are no mice in this house, if there were I'd get a cat!"

"Forget the damned mouse, you're avoiding the question! What are you up to?"

She inhaled deeply.

"Don't bother attempting a lie, Madam, I can peer into your thoughts should I choose to."

She hesitated. Could he really?

"Of course I can. Luckily for you, I comport myself as a gentleman and refrain from that intrusion. And besides, I don't have to. You're a terrible liar."

She let out her breath with an angry growl and slumped her shoulders. Eyes narrowed and diverted to the side, she crossed her arms in front of her and relented. "I've been looking for work."

"Why the devil would you do that?"

The room dimmed as a cloud formed in the otherwise clear sky and wandered in front of the sun. She glanced at the window. "For heaven's sake. You're very excitable for a ghost, do you know that?"

"I know no such thing and fail to see how that statement is relevant."

"Never mind. Isn't it obvious why I'm seeking employment? I promised to maintain this house, and that is no small task. Add to that two continually growing children who seem to require more food, clothing, and school supplies each year, and the small annuity my husband left me is quickly eaten away."

The cloud cleared and the room brightened. The added sense of warmth soothed over a portion of Adele's frayed nerves.

"Why didn't you ask for some assistance? I'm sure we can contrive a means for you to earn additional income without casting you out of the house to do it."

She hadn't asked because she didn't want to hear the myriad of reasons why she'd been foolish in agreeing to buy the house. This home was larger and much older than the one she'd lived in with her husband and came with a good deal of upkeep she hadn't experienced in her previous home. Her initial calculations of domestic expenses were sound, but she'd never thought to consider the structural or external maintenance of the home. Those items resided solely in the husband's domain; her monthly allotment was meant for the inside of the home. The lack of a husband, and the consequences thereof, only settled down upon her after the purchase of the house and she no longer had a landlord to appeal to. Ignoring these thoughts which had plagued her for several months already, she focused on the latter portion of the captain's question.

"I've already considered tasks which might keep me home. I have no space for a boarder—"

"I wouldn't allow one in any case."

"I have no skill for sewing or cooking, which is why I haven't the heart to let Bessie go…"

"It would be a folly if you do. She's far better suited to those tasks. She's a hearty woman, bred to the hearth and home. A refined lady ought not to sully her hands with common daily tasks."

She couldn't refrain from rolling her eyes. "Unfortunately, whatever skills a refined woman ought to have are not in high demand, which has led me to the newspaper." Accentuating her point, she took up the paper again and snapped it smartly before shielding herself with it.

"Why don't you take up the pen?"

Shields apparently hold no power against immaterial beings.

"Writing can be done from home," The Captain persisted.

"I haven't the imagination for it."

"You don't need imagination, I have a lifetime's worth of tales I can dictate to you, all guaranteed to keep an audience riveted."

"Yes, and I shudder to think what sort of tales those might be."

"There's no shame in having lived a man's life, and what does the content matter so long as you secure a writing position with a publication? Or better yet, we can put together a book, an instant best seller."

"Positions within a press are all but non-existent for women, especially writing positions. A book would take far too long to put together."

"Use a male pseudonym. And what does it matter the time so long as it brings back a respectable income?"

"The time matters very much if it stretches beyond my ability to buy food for my children."

"The idea is still preferable to you seeking employment outside the home. That's no occupation for a lady."

"Your thought process is archaic, Captain. Women from all walks of life can be found in outside careers these days."

"I fail to see how that makes it any more agreeable."

She buried her nose in the paper, patience at an end. "You're interrupting my search, Captain."

"Good."

This time she set the paper down with enough force to rattle the china and cutlery. "If I agree to take down your stories in the evenings, will you refrain from continuing this commentary? If your idea is successful, the added work will only prove temporary. It may in any case as I couldn't ask Bessie to take on monitoring the children in addition to the housework. But the children will be spending most of the summer with their grandmother, which makes now the best time for me to attempt working."

The air crackled with silence, and she held her breath.

"I suppose that might be agreeable."

"Oh, good."

"But mind I will hold you to your agreement to take down my tales in the evenings. I shall show no mercy and offer no quarter should you find yourself weary at the end of the day."

"Yes, yes, fine. Now, will you please leave me in peace?"

"And here begins the downfall of mankind. When once a woman contemplates leaving her natural place as ruler and keeper of the hearth, she becomes intolerable! Very well, Madam, you may have your so-called peace and suffer all the more for it!"

A strong wind rushed along the outside of the house, rattling the leaves in the tree beside the dining room, but a moment later it calmed. Adele peered about the room, but the peculiar essence the space took on in the captain's presence had lifted. The room shone light and bright and a hint too quiet. Rolling back her shoulders, she lifted her paper, assuring herself she had the right to exult in her triumph. Oddly, the remaining adverts failed to encourage her interest and she soon folded the paper and set it aside. Removing her uneaten breakfast and dishes to the kitchen, she resolved to find Bessie and see if there might be a task or two she could help with.

∼

"Honestly, Adele, I wish you would swallow your pride and come back to us."

Adele straightened in her seat at a cafe overlooking the harbor. Her mother-in-law sat across from her, sipping at her coffee and poking a fork at the remnants of her slice of cake with pursed lips.

Out on the water, small fishing boats dotted the waves closer inland as they made their way toward the horizon while larger ships, both steam and sail, crisscrossed the scene with the straight-forward bearing of vessels with definite destinations and timetables. She idly thought how much more she would enjoy being on one of those ships at that moment than sitting across from her mother-in-law.

"I worried from the start when you insisted upon leaving, and I still don't quite understand how or why you managed to acquire that odd house, but you see now it wasn't a good decision. It's stretched your funds too thin. You really should have taken that into consideration."

Adele ground her teeth. Her mother-in law had never managed a household's finances a day in her life. That task fell first to her husband, then her son, and finally to her daughter. "I assure you, mother, I took as many factors to heart as possible, but one can never predict all eventualities of a new venture. You'll recall, also, my stipend from Henry is quite small."

"I'm sure my dear boy provided quite decently for you and the children dear, you needn't wax defensive. I certainly don't hold it against you, running a household is a sizable chore for the best of us, but you've had your experimentation now and it's really time to come back to your senses."

"What an insufferable barnacle!" The captain's voice barged into her thoughts, causing her to jump.

"Good heavens, child," Mrs. Monroe's eyes widened. "Are you well? I worry the stress of this isolation you've put yourself into is too much for you."

"I'm perfectly fine, mother," she insisted through clenched teeth. "A draft at my neck is all, it's better now."

Stay out of this! She thought viciously as her husband's mother looked at her askance.

"Your mother-in-law can neither see nor hear me, there's no danger in voicing my commentary."

Adele rubbed at her eyes with one hand.

"There, you see?" Mrs. Monroe tsked. "Obviously unwell, you can't hide it from me. That's what comes of working outside the home. I insist you put in your regrets immediately and come back home."

"Finally, the wind-bag blows some sense."

"I am perfectly hale, mother, and have barely even begun my work." That was true. She'd managed to acquire a position as secretary to a local religious society but had barely been introduced to her work as of yet. Her first true shift was slated for later in the week.

"It's not becoming of a lady to work outside the home," her mother-in-law whined, resorting to a small pout and childlike expression of discontent when she found her overbearing insistence ineffectual. "If you will not think of your own reputation and that of your family name, at least consider the children!"

"There is no negative impact to the children, mother, I assure you they are perfectly content and entrenched in their studies."

"Which is another concern. They cannot possibly be getting an adequate education in this backwater!"

"What a presumptuous old barge!"

Quiet

"She can't hear me."

But I can and would rather not!

"Let me conjure up a gale. I'll see it blows her right back to the train station."

Don't you dare!

"Are you listening to me, Adele?"

Adele blinked across to the expectant wide eyes of the elder woman. Hang it. She'd been asked a question. This three-way conversation was proving too complicated for her already frayed nerves. She refused to admit her uncertainty about taking work after so adamantly arguing for the right to. "I appreciate your concerns, mother, but again, I assure you we are all quite well."

"Why don't you reconsider and come out with the children at the summer holidays? Do you remember Dr.

Walton? I heard from Hattie the other day he's also recently widowed. I'm sure the two of you—"

"Dr. Walton is a drunk and a morphine addict, I have no desire to associate with him."

"You do the man a disservice and show poor breeding to voice such gossip, Adele, I'm surprised at you! And this in thanks for my trying to help—"

"I have not asked for your help, I do not need your help, and I do not wish for your help." Adele snapped in an entirely uncharacteristic fashion. At her wits' end, she could stomach no further interference from either her mother-in-law or Captain Daniels. Why should it be so incomprehensible that she should be capable of supporting herself and her children? She would prove it to the both of them if it killed her!

"Well! Of all the ungrateful—" Mrs. Monroe stood to leave, her features splotched with anger. On any other day Adele would have felt instant remorse for her words, but she was far beyond caring about the woman's preferences today and all but stared her down as she continued. "Very well, if that's how you feel. I warn you, though, don't try to come begging my forgiveness. You've made your bed now, understand? Don't try it."

"I won't."

Her mother-in-law's eyes all but bulged from their sockets and her jaw dropped in disbelief. Flustered, she gathered her belongings and rustled away toward the train station in a cloud of black tulle. A devoted mother, in her own mind at least, she still wore full mourning for her only son.

"That's my girl!" Captain Daniels shouted with glee. "Were I human again I would kiss you. That was brilliant! I'm quite proud of you."

She stumbled over her thoughts, unexpectedly disconcerted by the suggestion of a kiss from the captain. Blinking, she forgot she'd been just as outraged at him for his outdated patriarchal views. "Well, that makes one of us. How terrible of me, I don't know what came over me."

"Good sense came over you, that's what. You're quite right to set a course on your own. You're far better off and perfectly capable of it."

That took her aback. "If you think so, why have you been making the same argument all this time?"

"I haven't made the same argument."

"Yes, you have. You don't want me to work either."

"Not wanting you to work is different from believing you incompetent. I hold no such belief."

She considered his words long enough to develop a fear of not living up to them. "What if she's right?" She whispered. "What if I'm just steering myself and my children into a storm?"

"Here, now, belay that kind of thinking, Adira."

"My name is Adele."

"And mine is Gregory, yet you refuse to use it. No,

after that display your name is no longer Adele. You've shown nothing but resilience from the moment you arrived here, and asserting yourself just now proved your crowning glory. Your name ought to befit a warrioress, and that is how I shall envision you from now on. Never doubt your strength, my dear."

CHAPTER 7

"Oh, there you are, Adele!" Mrs. Patterson, the mayor's wife, glided up to her where she stood beside a reception table. The older woman wore a slate-blue tea gown trimmed with white lace which managed to compliment both her gray hair and the most recent fashion plates. Adele hadn't realized when she applied to the secretarial position it would put her to work in the mayor's home but supposed now it made sense. Women of higher status were expected to keep themselves busy with philanthropic and humanitarian causes, after all.

"Have you finished with the registration forms?" The woman asked excitedly. "I'm curious to see the final attendance numbers. This is an excellent turnout! We must have over half the ladies of the Cove here!" Her features took on the glee of a little girl as Adele handed her the stack of papers she'd just completed sorting.

"That's wonderful, Mrs. Patterson," Adele smiled. "The lecture series you've arranged is bound to be a success."

Indeed, the mayoral home swarmed with the best society the little town had to offer, though Adele questioned if that were due to actual interest in the theme or curiosity. Mrs. Patterson had taken it upon herself to institute a club of sorts related to modern religious and intellectual themes she encountered in Boston. Hiring Adele as secretary went hand in hand with organizing a series of public events over the summer.

"We're nearly ready to start," Mrs. Patterson continued, still thumbing through pages. "Dr. Harris arrived a few minutes ago and is preparing his presentation. I'll be herding everyone into the dining room shortly." The dining room being the largest in the home, its contents were rearranged to accommodate several rows of chairs. "Feel free to peek in from the back if you'd like to hear the presentation, it's quite riveting and informative. There won't be any need to remain out here, just be sure to man the refreshment table during the intermission and after the lecture."

"Of course, Mrs. Patterson." Adele assured her, though now that she had official tasks to perform, she felt a measure of anxiety and hoped she wouldn't disappoint her new employer.

The woman flitted away as suddenly as she appeared, leaving Adele to make a final check of the table before following along behind the crowd headed to the presentation room. The topic for the night was indeed one of interest she was keen on hearing.

"A Theosophical Society chapter?" Captain Daniels made his presence known with a hint of annoyed disbelief. "This is where you've found work? Good heavens, woman, must I retract my statements against your mother-in-law?"

"Theosophy has been a rising thought movement and religion for decades, Captain, there's nothing untoward about it."

"Except that it professes to explain laws of nature which man has no way of knowing and ought not to pretend a claim on."

"Don't all religions do the same?"

"I maintain the same argument against all of them. Humans are forever attempting to place themselves in the position of divine creator and that can lead to no good whatsoever."

"I don't disagree with you, Captain, but please recall I'm not a member of this society, I'm an employee. I am tasked with filing paperwork and maintaining the refreshments, and I mean to do so."

"Very well, and do you intend to sit in on the lecture?"

"I had a mind to, yes, I admit I'm curious." She halted

in front of the door leading to the dining room, nudging it open a crack to observe the activity inside.

"What's the topic then?"

"Reincarnation."

"Damnation."

"This could be entertaining, Captain. I will ask you for your commentary later. Please refrain from providing it during the presentation or I won't be able to concentrate. I've heard the speaker is highly accomplished in his vocation." Seeing the women settling into their places, Adele maneuvered around the door as unobtrusively as possible and found an empty corner to occupy at the back of the room.

"The vocation of being a charlatan?"

She took a breath to reply, then snapped her mouth shut, belatedly remembering not to openly speak to the man no one in the room, including her, could see. *Reserve your judgment until after you've heard him speak. He's very well regarded in these circles. Mrs. Patterson has been gushing about how lucky we are to have him here visiting.*

"I'm willing to bet her enthusiasm is misplaced."

She ignored his comment, focusing instead on Mrs. Patterson, materializing from the opposite door leading to the kitchen and moving to the front of the room to deliver an eloquent introduction speech. By the end of it, every lady in attendance balanced on the edge of her seat in anticipation of the lecture.

Amid a round of applause another figure appeared from the kitchen, a man approaching his middling years who still retained a good measure of youthful vitality and handsomeness. His impeccable dress complimented the refinement of Mrs. Patterson's ensemble, and an easy smile instantly captured the ladies' attentions.

Within moments of beginning his lecture, Adele could easily understand why the man was so sought after. The information, in itself vast and fraught with terms new to Adele, took on properties of dramatic legend and indisputable scientific fact presented through the lens of a unique speaking style. Dr. Harris combined the active argumentation of a politician with refined charm to mesmerizing effect. By the end of the lecture, Adele's mind buzzed with unanswered questions, but she would have no opportunity to voice them as the crowd dispersed to the refreshment table. She was kept busy for the remainder of the afternoon.

"Don't tell me he drew you in with that drivel," the captain barked as she absently brushed out her hair at her dressing table later that evening.

"I don't deny the speech was well presented and the theme interesting, but was it truly drivel? You would know."

"Against my better judgment, I admit there is some basis to truth in what he spoke of. Departed souls can and do choose to return to earth at times."

"If the information was true, why do you berate it's believers so?"

"Because they are fluffing up their sense of importance based on half-understandings. There is a fundamental flaw in the idea of reincarnation as presented by your Dr. Harris."

"And what is that?"

"Humans think of all things in terms of linear time, but linear time does not exist. There is only existence. What you view as the past and the future are all concurrent within the present."

"But how can that possibly be?"

"The universe, and therefore the afterlife, does not function through the rules and dictates of people. People are no more significant in the grand scheme of the cosmos than the ants you trod upon daily without realizing. I cannot possibly explain it to you accurately because there are no human words to express it. It is beyond comprehension."

"You were human once, or I suppose several times, how are you able to comprehend it?"

"I did not in that state. My current state is vastly different. There is a kind of... permeability in existence within this dimension, there is no need to verbalize understanding, it's just... understood."

"Dimension?"

"Yes, the plane of existence on which we find

ourselves. You have yours, which you view as linear and solitary, but there are many others."

"I don't understand."

"Think of it this way, you are at your current point because of the decisions you made in your past, correct?"

"Yes."

"Well, at every point in life when a decision existed to be made, what if every decision were made?"

"What?" Adele scrunched her brow, hairbrush paused in midair. She thought she'd been following the captain's commentary fairly well, but lost the thread with the last statement.

"For example, you are a widow now because you chose to marry. What if you had rejected your husband's proposal, or married another? In each of those cases you would have led a different life, and my argument is that you are living that other life. In a different dimension, concurrently with this one."

"That's unimaginable!"

"Exactly. It is beyond the comprehension of your current reality, but in reality, whatever decision you focus on becomes your reality, you are the creator of it."

"This is far too confusing."

"I warned you it would be."

"And why are you here? You said you exist in a different reality, so how is it you can communicate with me here?"

"These realities are layered, my dear, and as my

dimension allows me the capability of understanding this, I can therefore breach the veil between the two."

"All this is going to give me a headache," Adele admitted with a yawn, setting down her hairbrush and making her way to bed. "It's very fascinating, but I think I'd prefer to keep my focus on only one dimension at a time."

"A wise decision, Adira."

~

The mayor's house all but echoed in the wake of each lecture. Since Adele's time before the presentations usually consisted of supervising in the kitchen or greeting attendees in the front foyer, she never saw the house in an empty state to begin with. The consequent expansion of space after each event astounded her. Given they'd only just completed the second lecture, she supposed the novelty would wane in time.

Dr. Harris would be in residence for eight weeks, facilitating multiple talks and courses during that time. Adele shook her head. The thought of so much responsibility reminded her of all the social clubs her mother and sister-in-law insisted she take part in and caused her to shudder. An amiable and sociable fellow like Dr. Harris was much better suited to such a life.

She set the final handful of cups and glasses she'd been

collecting from where they'd been set by attendees on the refreshment table. The housekeeper would complete the tidying. With a nod, she made a final turn of the room, scanning for missed items, then exited toward the front foyer.

"You must be Mrs. Monroe," a voice greeted her from the direction of the parlor as she passed it. She jumped in her march, unaware anyone aside from her remained in the house. Mrs. Patterson had seen her guests to the door, leaving with the last and instructing Adele to leave at her discretion once the dining room was put to rights. Wheeling about, she caught sight of Dr. Harris grinning from the doorway.

"Oh, hello Dr. Harris. Forgive me, I wasn't aware you were still here. Yes, I'm Mrs. Monroe."

"I knew it could be no other, your auric field is radiant, I'm quite pleased with Mrs. Patterson's decision to hire you on."

"Oh?" She failed to comprehend how the doctor's opinion made much difference in her employment, but given Mrs. Patterson's devoted support of him, she assumed this additional praise could only be helpful to her. It indeed it was praise. "My auric field?"

"Yes, I noticed it immediately during my lecture on reincarnation and had to inquire about you with Mrs. Patterson, I hope you forgive me the presumption."

"Yes, of course." Her cheeks warmed. He'd noticed her during the last lecture? "I'm happy to be of assistance to Mrs. Patterson and am finding your presentations very informative."

Unused to any sort of male attention and worried she might reverse his good humor if she began attempting discussion of themes she claimed no knowledge of, she darted a glance toward the front door.

"How remiss of me," the doctor proclaimed, exaggerated worry furrowing his brow. "Am I keeping you from something?"

"Oh, well, I—"

"Why don't you allow me to escort you to your next destination? Is it far? Shall I retrieve my car?"

"I couldn't possibly inconvenience you."

"It's no inconvenience at all, I assure you."

Uncertain, Adele narrowly prevented herself from chewing at her bottom lip. "Well, the car would be more convenient as I live on upper Mariner's Lane, one of the further homes from the town center."

"It's settled then," Dr. Harris graced her with a wide grin. "I'll be out front in a blink." Stepping toward the door, he turned the handle and offered an elegant bow as he opened it and indicated she should precede him. Adele gave a small smile.

His blatantly overdone movements served the purpose of setting her at ease. She couldn't recall ever having met such an informally charming man. Shutting the door behind them, he saluted her with a touch to his hat brim before making his way around the side of the house toward the garage.

"Tell me Mrs. Monroe," Dr. Harris began once they were seated in the car and headed toward Mariner's Lane. "Are you a long-time student of Theosophy? If so, it's a wonder we haven't crossed paths before this."

"Oh, no, I've heard of the thought movement in passing, but never had the opportunity to explore it myself until recently." She stole a glance at his profile. This was the closest she'd been to the man since his arrival, and she began to understand why so many of the ladies were enthralled with him. The lines of his features ran as smoothly as an artist's pencil and his thick, lustrous hair hinted at admirable waves.

"How unfortunate for our cause, you bring such vital energy to a room." He turned his head briefly to grin at her, eyes sparkling as though he knew she'd been observing him.

A blush bloomed across her cheeks, and she feigned interest in the landscape outside the window. "I'm sure you exaggerate."

"Not at all. I'm not speaking of energy in the ambiguous terms so many unenlightened souls use, but of a discernible essence so vibrant as to be instantly recognizable." He held her gaze as long as possible given the constraint of needing to watch the road. "To those with an awakened sense of sight of course." He added after returning his attention to the road.

"Such as you."

"Yes, exactly."

Adele weighed his words. Their meaning lacked in solidity as far as her limited and traditional vocabulary was concerned, but he spoke them with such conviction. That alone compelled her to treat them as meaningful. "I'm afraid such a concept is difficult for me to understand."

"Only because you haven't been properly initiated into the education of it. Perhaps—" the words cut off sharply.

"Yes?" She prompted.

"I am compelled to take you on as a student in these matters. "Yes, I am quite sure the higher powers wish it to be so."

Student? Higher powers? Adele might indulge in a bit of fanciful observation of the doctor, but her sensibilities were quite certain she should not take on such an intimate interaction with a man she really didn't know all that well. "That is very kind of you, but—"

"I can't possibly withstand a refusal from you," he insisted as the car pulled up alongside the fence of her home and he shut off the engine. Turning in his seat, he fixed her with a look of utter seriousness. "You shall be my greatest masterpiece. Say yes, do say yes." To emphasize his words, he took hold of her hand, trapping it between both of his. "We can begin this very day, this very moment. Why don't I stay for coffee?"

"Well—" Adele stared at their hands, intent upon giving a small tug to reestablish her hand's freedom. Before she could formulate a polite response, excited shouts drew her attention to the front steps of her house, down which her children came running. Dr. Harris dropped her hand.

"Ah, I see the atmosphere will not be at all studious. Please take my offer into consideration and think on arranging some private time for such a worthy cause. I shall await your answer at our next meeting."

Exiting the car, he walked around to open her door and offer his hand. The children bounded up to hug her and she would have introduced them to Dr. Harris, had he not already returned to his seat and started the car's engine by the time she looked up. He sent an abbreviated wave behind the glass of the windshield and set the car into motion.

"Who was that, mother, someone from your work?" her son asked, craning his neck to follow the descent of the car. Cars fascinated the boy and she smiled, shaking her head when his lack of attention to his own destination nearly saw him walking headlong into the banister on the porch steps.

"Yes, that's Dr. Harris."

"Why didn't he stay?"

"I suppose he had somewhere else to be."

"Will he bring you home every day?"

"Certainly not."

"Sometimes?" The boy's eyes still scanned the road, now devoid of any cars.

"Perhaps."

The contemplation gave her pause. Did she want the doctor escorting her home? Her sense of propriety notwithstanding, she had to admit a small thrill of excitement at the prospect.

CHAPTER 8

"I find him quite charming."

Dr. Harris hadn't surrendered his insistence on meeting privately with Adele. If anything, he'd become more adamant and persuasive. She relented once the summer holidays began, and she'd seen her children packed safely to their grandmother. Not that she eschewed all propriety. Their lessons generally consisted of chats in Mrs. Patterson's parlor, with the matron's approval. They'd only met a few times in the past weeks, but she'd grown fond of him during that time. He showed an inordinate amount of caring in his compliments and she was quite convinced now of his sincerity.

"And here I thought you had some sense." Captain Daniels grumbled.

"I do. I don't find you at all charming." The roll of a summer thunderstorm rumbled across the harbor. "All right, I amend my statement. I don't find you charming when you are being petty."

"I am never petty. There's something unsavory about that charlatan, and you are proving just female enough in your sentiments that I worry you may be deceived by him."

"You offer me very little credit, Captain, I thought you crowned me an Amazon?"

"And so I did. And so I do. A woman capable of withstanding the fiercest gale one might sail into maneuvering around the Cape of Good Hope. However, in matters of the heart the female of the species has a habit of showing remarkably poor taste."

"As evidenced by the string of broken hearts I'm sure you left in every port, am I right?"

"We are not discussing my ports of call, Madam, we are discussing your poor judgment. Kindly stay the course."

"My apologies."

"Now, where were we?"

"We were ending the conversation due to the fact it's not your business what I feel or don't feel for Dr. Harris."

"It is my business when it effects my home."

"And how exactly does my employment effect your home, other than to maintain it?"

"I refuse to allow that con artist into the place on grounds of questionable moral character and know that at this rate you'll be inviting him to tea within the week."

"You're overworking yourself, Captain."

"Furthermore, if you will not take my preferences into account, think of your children."

"My children? What have you got to say about my children? And mind you think carefully on your response, Captain."

"They're not too terrible for landlubbing brats I suppose, in fact they've rather impressed me with their shows of reason and exemplary comportment."

Adele opened her mouth in preparation of berating the captain on the topic of his agreement to abstain from wandering the house.

"Observed from afar, Madam, I have not forsaken our agreement. The children are as yet salvageable and may grow into respectable adults, but they are in a highly impressionable state. You ought to take care about the influences you allow to surround them."

"I assure you, Captain, I take every such care. What makes you so certain Dr. Harris is deceptive? Can you make a comparison with any true seer?"

"As a matter of fact, I can."

"Of course, you can. Do tell, this ought to be entertaining."

"Enlightening more likely. It was 1871; my crew and I made port in the Arabian Gulf and as we'd completed our business with the local merchants early, I made the poor decision to allow a few additional hours of leave. I was still young then, hadn't learned better. Well, one of the merchants informed me as I was collecting a personal commission of pearls that the Turks were reasserting their presence in the area. I decided it would be best to sail out sooner than later. That meant, of course, I had to track down my crew. I found most of them in the usual places serving up food, drink, and diversion, but there was a group still missing. After enlisting the aid of a few local urchins, I found them, hanging on the predictions of a fortune teller."

"I've heard sailors are notoriously superstitious."

"Seamen, Madam! And yes, they are. However, I don't believe that was the draw in this case. The fortune teller in question was young and very pretty. Unfortunately, my arrival ensured she would not benefit from her work. My men would have ignored the regional mandate that such fortunes are not to be paid for, but had no means of doing so once I arrived."

"What a shame!"

"Indeed, but there was no help for it. I ushered them out, but before I could follow, the woman grabbed hold of my arm and her eyes took on an other-worldly glow. She told me I would meet her twice in her lifetime but only once in mine."

"How peculiar."

"It was more than peculiar, Madam, it was damned terrifying! That look in her eyes spoke of active transit across dimensions, though I had no idea about dimensions at the time.

When it faded, she must have realized the loss of income my arrival incurred and looked so lamentable as to cause me a moment of regret. I paid her for the service of keeping my men entertained and easier to find, then on a whim extracted the pearl necklace from my pocket and gave that to her as a gift. Most foolhardy thing I've ever done, that necklace was an expensive commission."

"Perhaps it was the universal power forcing you into kindness just to spite you. That was an interesting story, Captain, but what does it have to do with Dr. Harris?"

"Were you not listening? The look in that woman's eyes! Enough to evoke the fear of the Almighty, precisely because it was a connection to the supernatural. The demeanor is fearsome and humbling, not blank."

"Dr. Harris' eyes are not blank."

"They were when they made that hogwash pronouncement about your aura."

Adele started, having all but forgotten her first conversation with the doctor. "Captain, I must insist you refrain from eavesdropping on my personal conversations! How am I to go about life always fearing you're lurking around every corner? It's not becoming of a gentleman!" Here she paused, thinking back to that day and her curiosity.

The energy fields had come up in conversation a time or two since then, and she'd found them most intriguing. She liked thinking of herself as awash in beauteous colors. "Are auras not real, then?" She held her breath, thinking she'd be grandly disappointed if they weren't.

"They are real." Captain Daniels assured her in a more moderate tone. "His claim to be able to see yours was not."

"Because it doesn't shine as he said?"

"Your blasted aura shines like a damnable beacon!" he roared, then calmed again. "That's the problem. And as to that snake oil salesman, he doesn't see your aura because he hasn't got the damned inner sight to be able to! Very few humans do."

"If I shine so brightly, why is that a problem?"

"Because you are far too innocent in the ways of the world. You will attract every deceptive soul within a hundred-mile radius to take advantage of you."

She bristled. "Again, you give me too little credit. I am a widow and mother and well over thirty. I'm not so innocent as you presume."

"My darling Adira, the age of your body is no indication of the age of your soul. You are still wide-eyed and adventurous on that front. In a way I envy that in you. But you cannot argue your life experience is limited, despite the milestones you've crossed."

"Very well, I won't. That doesn't change the fact you are not my protector, Captain. I must make my own way in the world and learn my own lessons, mustn't I?"

"You say that now, you'll sing a different tune once left to your own devices."

"Try me."

~

THE AFTERNOON of Mrs. Patterson's Theosophical Society luncheon proved exceptionally perfect in terms of mildness and visual aesthetic. Temperatures remained manageable with slight breezes of infant strength rustling leaves and swaying flowers.

The ladies wandered the garden while their meal was arranged under an open-sided tent erected on the lawn. Adele supervised yet again, taking pride in her growing proficiency in hostessing on a large scale. She'd learned the rudiments as a young woman, but her own home saw few guests during her marriage.

Satisfied all appeared perfect, she nodded to the housekeeper, who rang a triangle to announce the meal. Like bees alighting from a field to swarm their way home, the society ladies obediently began to emerge from the garden. To counter the motion, Adele moved toward the garden. She wouldn't be needed again until after the meal and had been staring at the beautiful blooms since her arrival that day. Finding the paving stones leading visitors through the main regions of the garden, she followed them around the house and out of sight of the luncheon tent.

"You've been avoiding me, my pet." A now familiar

voice hailed from behind her soon after beginning her stroll. She turned to smile at Dr. Harris.

"No, I haven't. You draw quite a crowd, especially given your limited engagement schedule here. It's been terribly busy for me and Mrs. Patterson." She meant it teasingly, though she did wonder again at the doctor's apparent lack of realization about how much labor went into preparing for his speeches. Then again, she supposed he wasn't privy to most of it. He tended to arrive mere moments before his lecture and either depart before or disappear during the cleaning process.

"Have you thought about my request?" He took her elbow and led her toward a small arbor harboring a stone bench.

She sighed. But a few days prior, he'd announced to her she excelled so expediently at her studies with him she must accompany him on the remainder of his New England tour as his personal secretary. The offer jolted her, and for a moment she found herself so caught up in his enthusiasm she nearly agreed. Providentially, an image of her children flashed across her mind's eye, bringing her back to rational thought. "I have, but I'm sorry to say I don't see how I'd be able to manage it."

"My pet, this is your divine calling, you must manage it!"

She furrowed her brow at his words. It seemed to her a divine calling ought to call the person it's meant for, not a third party. Until he'd mentioned it, she'd never considered traveling away from her newfound home. "I can't, I assure you, it was difficult enough for me to take the time away to help Mrs. Patterson with the society, and my children are still in need of me for—"

"Just like a mother to think she is ever needed," Dr. Harris protested, crossing his arms in front of him and taking on a petulant demeanor. "I'm sure there is someone else in your home who could care for them, isn't there?"

She blinked up at him. Surely by now he was aware of her widowed status. They hadn't directly discussed it, but... "Forgive me, but, I assumed you were aware I am a widow."

He raised his brows at her. "Of course I am, silly girl, but what has that to do with my statement? Surely you have a maid or housekeeper present in your home?"

Adele's jaw drifted open. Could he possibly believe all homes came equipped with such personnel? "Dr. Harris,"

"And that's the next thing, why do you insist on such formality? I must have told you a thousand times by now my name is Avery."

Now he looked perturbed. She relented, hoping it might help him focus on the discussion at hand. "Avery, I cannot possibly hand over the upbringing of my children to the housekeeper."

"They'll be none the worse for it, that's how it's done in countless households around the globe. Honestly, pet, why are you so resistant? Do you not care for me? Because all this time I could swear you did."

"Well, I... we're not discussing—"

"Of course we are! What do you suppose I meant by inviting you to travel with me? To arrange my meals and schedule?"

"But you said you needed a secretary—"

"And what is a secretary but a man's right hand? The complimentary half to form the whole? I couldn't possibly form such an intimate bond with someone I don't deeply care for."

Adele's head swam. True, she hadn't been completely ignorant of his interest in her, but such an admission was too sudden. "I didn't realize—"

"Oh, my little pet," he chuckled. "You truly are a child, aren't you?"

She stiffened her spine. "Please excuse me, Dr. Harris, I ought to get back to the luncheon. Standing, she made to walk in that direction, but Harris blocked her way and took her by the elbows, bemused by her show of temper.

"Come now, don't be cross, I only have your best interests in mind after all. You must understand how terribly frustrating it is for me to witness you ignoring your gift. You are such a vibrant soul, you know." His words dipped into a near whisper and he stepped in close to her, leaning toward her until his breath warmed her earlobe. She stood for a moment cocooned by him, the rest of the world hidden from her perception.

"I'm afraid I don't know that," she admitted without confidence. "You keep speaking of my soul and my energy as tangible things, but I can't fathom such things."

"You will," he whispered again, then leaned back far enough to bring one hand up to caress her cheek. "With the proper training. Do you know, my soul recognized yours in an instant?"

"It did?" She swayed toward him.

"Of course, but such is the way of things when two like energies have found each other. It is the essence of the cosmos. Two halves realizing that together they form a more significant whole. Twin flames. Soulmates. That's what we are, my pet, surely you realize it."

"I'm quite sure I saw them wander this way... Dr. Harris? Dr. Harris?!" Mrs. Patterson's shrill call sounded across the garden.

Dr. Harris all but shoved her over the bench and into the back corner of the arbor as he stepped out into the open garden. Clouds of annoyance flitted over his features an instant before he put on a dazzling smile.

"There you are!" Mrs. Patterson came into view from around the bend in the walking path, raising one hand in a wave while the other tugged up the hem of her skirt. "Oh, and I see Mrs. Monroe is with you, how perfect as I would have been searching for her next. It's time for your farewell address to close the luncheon, and then I've got quite the exciting suggestion to discuss with you." She panted slightly as she neared, the exertion of a garden stroll being more than she was accustomed to. "Mrs. Brisby brought it up and it sparked an instant vision in my head. I thought I must share it with you, it cannot wait."

Pausing in her cryptic recitation, she peered over at Adele. "Mrs. Monroe, do be a dear and see that all the final dishes are gathered and begin setting out the ladies' coats and shawls, will you?"

"Yes, of course, Mrs. Patterson."

"Thank you, dear, you are an invaluable help to me."

Adele raced from the garden, battling a dizzying imbalance brought on by a barrage of conflicting emotions.

CHAPTER 9

The work of seeing guests out, collecting and organizing commentary cards, and generally ensuring all got put back to rights following the luncheon provided Adele much needed time to calm her thoughts and nerves. Dr. Harris' words replayed in her mind. Her heart fluttered at the beauty of them, however poorly delivered, but her mind argued the probability of a man forming such strong attachment to her over only a few weeks. Then again, her fondness for him had grown quickly as well, and so close on the heels of her mourning. A stab of guilt assaulted her, but she bypassed it via an impromptu comparison of both men. After some dedicated thought, she determined her feelings to be at least as warm toward Dr. Harris as they had been toward her husband. In which case she must surely be in love.

She paused in ascending the back steps to the house,

knitting her brows together. How did one truly understand if their feelings constituted love? She experienced love to and from her family, which differed from romantic love of course. She knew the love of a mother for her children, but that also differed. And she could make no other comparison with unrelated men. Well, unless she counted the captain, the only other male presence she'd spent any length of time with.

Her interactions with him were of an altogether different nature. The contentment she felt in his presence, the distinct, comforting heaviness of the air even when they were not in active conversation, that constituted nothing more than an atmospheric effect. The sense of security and unseen protection, the certainty that no harm could come to her as she moved through her day at home and when she laid down to sleep at night, that only came of knowing a ghost could manipulate the surroundings. And the way the sound of his voice tickled and thrilled her, sending shivers over her skin... The way his compliments smoothed over her with the sensuality of warm honey, that was... Well, she didn't know what that was.

"There you are, Mrs. Monroe!" Mrs. Patterson poked her head out from the double doors on the back porch and smiled at her. "You must come in, Dr. Harris and I have an exciting prospect to discuss with you."

"With me?"

"Yes, come in, come in," she gestured with little gathering flaps of her hand. Adele complied, though she couldn't imagine what the mayor's wife and the doctor could possibly want to consult with her about.

"Please do sit," the older woman insisted once they reached the parlor. Dr. Harris already sat at one end of the sofa and smiled in Adele's direction when she moved to take the seat opposite him. Mrs. Patterson joined Dr. Harris on the other end of the sofa.

"I admit I've had an idea floating about in my head for several days which I meant to share with the doctor, and Mrs. Brisby's suggestion, of a similar nature, cemented my conviction that I must share it with Dr. Harris."

Adele nodded, still uncertain as to how this mysterious revelation related to her.

"Dr. Harris is quite agreeable and thinks it a marvelous addition to his lecture offerings, an authentic representation of several themes we've been discussing." The woman beamed and nodded at Dr. Harris, who smiled politely back.

"I'm sorry, Mrs. Patterson," Adele commented, "But I'm confused as to the nature of this offering. Are you adding a new lecture to the series?" She swung her gaze between the two people on the sofa, thoroughly confused.

Mrs. Patterson broke out in a subdued laugh. "Heavens, me, I'm so excited I haven't adequately explained things, have I? I'm speaking of a seance, my dear.

"A seance?"

"Yes, of course. Wouldn't it be the perfect exhibition to complement the lectures? A sort of grand finale in the days leading up to the farewell breakfast?"

The older woman's wide, expectant gaze prompted Adele into a response. "Yes, that does sound quite fitting." Though she wasn't as certain as her response would indicate. She'd heard of seances of course, and could recall periods when the elaborate rituals meant to commune with the dead had been in vogue, but she'd always regarded these events as somewhat suspect and unsavory.

"And you see," Dr. Harris added in, "why you must be intimately included in this event."

Adele blinked, again searching the faces of her companions in turn. "Forgive me, but no, I don't."

Mrs. Patterson chuckled. "Really, Mrs. Monroe? Have you forgotten your home has been considered the most fiercely haunted building this town has to offer for over a decade and a half?"

Adele's jaw dropped. Her home? She didn't want to consider the captain's reaction to such an event held in the house.

"Yes," Dr. Harris added in. "Mrs. Patterson has told me all about the place, I'm astounded you didn't do so yourself, Mrs. Monroe, terribly remiss of you. I understand an old sea captain killed himself in the place. It's perfect, absolutely perfect! Have you witnessed any spirit activity there yourself?" He leaned forward in his seat, piercing her with an assessing gaze.

She swallowed. "No, none at all, I fear the rumors of haunting must have been exaggerated."

"Well, no matter," the doctor slumped back in his seat with a frown. "Buildings which have witnessed death always boast some sort of spectral connection, which still makes your home optimal. The backstory will provide excellent atmosphere for guests."

"While I appreciate your interest and agree a seance sounds complimentary to the lecture themes," Adele addressed both her companions, "I'm afraid I couldn't possibly offer up my home."

"Why on earth not?" Dr. Harris exclaimed.

"I worry such a thing might frighten the children." Thankfully, Adele's children would be back in residence at the house by the final week of lectures.

"Oh, that's true," Mrs. Patterson nodded, pressing her lips together. "I'd forgotten about your children, do forgive me."

"It's quite all right."

"Can they not be sent away for a day or two?" Dr. Harris persisted.

"I'm afraid not. They've already spent a good deal of time away this summer and will be preparing for the resumption of their studies."

"Yes, you're right, it wouldn't do to disturb their routines so," Mrs. Patterson agreed. Though her children were long married and moved into their own homes, the woman hadn't lost her motherly sensibilities, to Adele's great relief. "Do forget we mentioned it." Then, turning to Dr. Harris, "well, it was a fine thought, but I can easily offer up my home for the purpose."

Dr. Harris looked none too pleased at the development but seeing that his one ally had turned against him, he relented and graced his hostess with a smile. "That would be gracious of you Mrs. Patterson. You have a talent for going far beyond the call of a hostess and I cannot adequately express my gratitude. I am indebted to you."

Mrs. Patterson blushed and offered some complimentary platitudes. The conversation diverted away from her home, there appeared no further reason for Adele to remain, so her employer ushered her out.

~

"Absolutely not!"

Adele rubbed her brow. The captain's vehemence set her brain to rattling in her skull and they'd already been arguing half an hour.

"You shall under no circumstances attend such a farce! I forbid it! Seance indeed."

"Captain, you are in no position to forbid me anything. Aside from that, I must attend. It is a condition of my employment that I am available for all Society events."

"Then you shall quit your employment, dammit. We

are close enough to completing my book, I'm sure we can find the means to keep you afloat until its publication."

"You're being unreasonable."

"I am never unreasonable, as I've assured you in the past."

Adele rolled her eyes. "Yes, so you have. On numerous occasions. Very well, if you believe your argument valid, kindly explain to me why. Since my arrival you've made it obvious that communion between the living and dead is possible. Why not encourage it formally?

Adele paced her room, moving out of habit toward the French doors and balcony. Bypassing the telescope, she opened the doors and stepped out, breathing in the warm sea air. She rested her hands on the balcony railing and peered out to the shoreline, smiling to herself. Little chance existed she would spot Bessie and the children somewhere along that strip of sand, but her eyes scanned for them anyway.

"Those with limited knowledge of the afterlife ought not to muddle with it," the captain's argument followed along, albeit more subdued. Perhaps that was the reason for her preference of seeking the balcony when they spoke. The familiar prickle at the nape of her neck and the barely perceptible press at her back, as though the captain stood behind her, ready to brace and embrace her if she should lean back. He always responded more calmly here, where he could easily observe the sea.

"Myself included." He continued. "At best, these

events are a stab in the dark dredging up an unknown soul who may or may not be pleased about it. At worst, they are a carnival show of deception meant to fleece an unsuspecting mourner. Mark my words, no good will come of it in either case."

"Avery assures me all precautions are taken to ensure a completely safe experience during a seance."

"Avery, is it?" The captain's voice regained a measure of hardness and the light press of the air receded at her back, sparking a moment of panic in Adele. "Heaven forbid I should contradict the all-knowing Avery."

"Why Gregory, I believe you're jealous."

The summer breeze stilled, the ships on the horizon seemed to pause in their voyage across a painted seascape.

"Preposterous. Human emotions are irrelevant to me, I should think by now you understand that."

"Quite so, my mistake," she soothed, smiling when the cocoon of his presence returned to surround her. Inhaling, she continued her argument. "In all honesty, aside from my responsibility to attend I'm rather curious about this seance."

"Why? What is it that intrigues you so about such a wretched display?"

"From what I understand, these events are conducted with the intention of drawing the spirit near enough to communicate with, is that correct?"

"Yes."

"Well," she hesitated, gnawing on her lip. "If the spirit is already close enough, would such an event be able to provide additional substance? I mean, for example, you speak to me often, is there no way to encourage you to present yourself in a more tangible form? There must be a way, people are always telling stories of seeing ghosts."

The breeze reasserted itself, invoking an agitated rustle in the canopy of leaves surrounding her. "Those restless souls require a great deal of energy to manifest in such a way," Captain Daniels explained. "That energy is generally connected to an intensity of harsh emotion. Anger, grief, fear. To encourage such a vision would be to invite disaster into a home, which is why I cannot agree to you attending a seance."

"What a shame, I often think it would be nice to have these talks with you and be able to see you as I did that first night."

"You saw me?"

She nodded. "In my dreaming. Was that odd?"

"I suppose not. The dreaming state is the closest humans come to the spirit world while living, the only time you can traverse the veil with as much ease as I can. I suppose I hadn't considered it. So few of you ever develop the ability to do so at will."

"I can learn to look for you in my dreams? What a marvelous thought." And it was, she realized, wondering why she hadn't made the connection herself earlier. If she could see the captain in her dreams, this phantom relationship could become more tangible. Perhaps she wouldn't be so harshly reminded of her solitary status each time she left home, knowing the night would bring a more lifelike closeness.

"You must not do so, my dear." The captain asserted, dashing her tiny spark of hope.

"Why not?"

"Because your attention ought to be in your own realm. You ought to be looking for companionship among the living."

Her heart sank at what felt like a blatant rejection. "I have companionship. I have Bessie and the children."

"All well and good, but I'm talking of something more substantial. Male companionship."

"And yet you disapprove of Dr. Harris."

"That man is an insincere snake, you deserve better."

"You have no proof of that." Her temper flared. "Your preferences contradict each other, Captain. You discouraged the thought of my marrying on the assertion that you are the master of this home, yet you disapprove of my desire to see you."

"Yes, I suppose you're right."

His admission stunned her. Adele couldn't recall another instance of the captain openly relinquishing ground in an argument. It jarred her inner sense of stability and made her heart ache.

"I was wrong to discourage you." He continued.

"You're still in the prime of youth, now is the time to enjoy the thrill and adventure of love."

"I'm thirty-three, that is nowhere near youth and far too old to interest any man."

"You are exactly in the age when a woman loses her girlish fancies and becomes interesting."

"Just not to you it appears. Or any man you might deem worthwhile. Captain, you have an amazing talent for instilling confidence in a woman." Whirling about, she marched back into the bedroom, slamming the doors behind her. Snatching up her hat from the dresser, she raced through the house to the front door.

Unsure whether she feared an apology from the captain or the withholding of one, she determined she hadn't the strength to face either possibility. She opted for a walk along the shore instead. A long walk until her legs ached and she was too tired to think anymore.

CHAPTER 10

The night of the seance arrived before Adele had any time to think more deeply on it and the captain's concerns. She'd been too distracted pondering the captain himself while attempting to convince herself she wasn't. This took the form of accepting additional invitations from Dr. Harris to spend time together outside of the Theosophical society events. A risky business considering he preferred not to spend the time out at some public cafe, instead inviting her to meals in a little seaside cottage he'd rented for his stay.

The space was secluded and serene, offering ample opportunities for evening strolls and hours' long conversation over nothing in particular. Dr. Harris showed an unwavering preoccupation with her at these times, stealing opportunities to hold her hand, embrace her, and even kiss her. Such attention startled her at first, but the initial concern over propriety her conscience attempted to conjure faded as she allowed herself to enjoy being cared for and wanted.

The passage of days also strengthened her understanding that the captain didn't care for her, at least not in any substantial way. He'd remained away since their argument, no longer joining her in the evenings to ask about her day. She'd put off continuing work on his manuscript, but the action failed to invoke any resurgence of his presence in the form of a disgruntled tirade. So, she diverted her attention, convincing herself by the night of the seance she had thoroughly forgotten the captain and that Dr. Harris must genuinely love her.

"Welcome, everyone, welcome!" Dr. Harris intoned from the staircase landing to the small crowd of women gathered in Mrs. Patterson's foyer. "I am grateful for your attendance and anticipate a spectacular display of the universal mysteries which we have so ardently decoded and studied in the past weeks." He descended the stairs, not pausing at the bottom but marching through the gaggle of women, who all wore expressions of awe as they hurried to clear themselves from his path.

He paused in front of the parlor door and turned to face them again. "I warn you, what you are about to witness may be frightening. It will cement for you truths which your soul may understand but your mind has yet to accept. It is highly likely one or several of you may be induced to a fit of emotional extreme. Sorrow, raptures, you may faint dead away. Rest assured, Mrs. Patterson and Mrs. Monroe have been advised on how best to console you in this case. You may enter in complete calm and security, but I must insist if any one of you still holds significant doubt as to your ability to participate, please see your way home now and I will happily greet you again at tomorrow's lecture reviewing these events." He waited while the women rustled in place, each looking to the other, one or two sparing a glance for the front door, but none of them venturing toward it.

"Excellent, ladies. Now, if you will all follow me inside and find a seat among those arranged near the table."

Adele followed behind, reminding herself of all the instructions Dr. Harris had provided her in recent days and darting a glance toward Mrs. Patterson to see if she showed any signs of nervousness which might reflect her own slightly uneasy stomach and restlessness. But the matron was too far away on the other side of the room to provide any overt indication, so Adele took her place at the far end of the observation chairs.

A small card table had been brought into the parlor and set near the windows, the drapes of which were now tightly drawn. On top of the black-clothed table sat a candelabra, the main source of light in the room. Dr. Harris previously explained that the electrical currents of modern lighting interfered with the conduction of otherworldly entities and messages. Beside the silver candelabra sat a small brass bell with a wooden handle and a modified ear trumpet, the narrowest quarter of which had been removed. One of the women approached the table with hesitant steps.

"Mrs. Barnes, welcome." Dr. Harris greeted her. "Have no fear, you are in competent hands. Please take a seat."

While planning the seance, Mrs. Patterson had asked if anyone would volunteer to attempt contact with a recently departed loved one. Mrs. Barnes was chosen from the small number of those who responded positively. The focus tonight would be to establish communication with a nephew who'd recently been lost to consumption.

The woman took the seat indicated, one of two chairs flanking the table. Dr. Harris sat in the other.

"As you can see," the doctor intoned as everyone settled and focused their collective attention on him. "We have lit the candles and offered them as the only light in this area of the house to facilitate the spirit's ability to locate us.

"Here," he lifted the bell and gave it an illustrative shake. "Is a bell, which I now place on the floor beside the table to provide the spirits a means of communication in the event they are unable to create sounds resembling vocalization."

He leaned down to set the bell on the floor to the rear of the table. He'd also explained that spirits often materialized first as a ground-hugging mist, so this provided easier access to the bell if the spirit were not strong enough to reach the height of the table.

"And finally," he concluded, holding up the cone of the ear trumpet, "A spirit cone to amplify the voices of the dead." He set the cone on its side on the table, the larger portion facing the observing women.

"Mrs. Barnes, would you please set your hands, palms down, on the table?"

The woman nodded and set her hands on the table. Dr. Harris set his hands on top of hers. "Take note of the weight of my hands upon yours, they serve to aid in connecting you to the universal current which flows through me. Now, if everyone would kindly close your eyes and breathe deeply."

The small space resounded with the sound of multiple inhaled breaths.

"Spirits of the great beyond, I call to you!" Dr. Harris asserted with strong and steady tones. "I seek one of your own, a recent journeyer to your realm, a Mr. John Barnes." Another collective inhalation. "John Barnes, do you hear me?"

A pause.

"Do you hear me, John Barnes? If you can hear me, make yourself known in this room."

The brass bell rang out and several women let out startled gasps. Adele's pulse quickened.

"John, your aunt would like to pose questions to you. Will you respond? Ring once for yes, twice for no."

The bell sounded once.

"You may ask your questions, Mrs. Barnes."

"Johnny," the woman began, a quaver in her voice. "Are you well? Are you free from pain now?"

One ring of the bell.

"Your mother says she feels your presence, have you been with her?"

One ring.

"Is the afterlife like what we've been taught? Airy and bright, up in the clouds?"

The bell rang once, then again. More gasps.

"Is it—"

Mrs. Barnes' question broke off as the bell began to ring again, this time urgently and erratically. Adele nearly jumped from her seat when the woman beside her grabbed her hand. Then the bell stopped as sharply as it began. An uneasy murmur drifted between the observing women as they looked to Dr. Harris for indication all was still well.

"An anomaly in the spiritual field, ladies. The recently departed often have difficulty maintaining their presence here. I will attempt to reestablish the connection." The doctor shut his eyes and took on a look of intense concentration before repeating his initial inquiry.

"John Barnes, are you here with us? If you are here, make your presence known! Give a sign that you are here!"

The bell began to ring erratically again, the flustered

women turning their heads to and fro, searching for any visible evidence of a spirit in the room. Adele too, searched the dark corners for specters. Her search was cut short, however, when the candelabra extinguished itself and the bell fell silent once again.

"Ladies," Dr. Harris announced into the dark, "I believe John Barnes' entry into the room may have brought with it additional entities which—"

A rattling took up against the wood flooring.

"The table!" screeched Mrs. Barnes. "It's shaking!"

All the women began to chatter at once, chairs scraping as they moved to rise despite the dark and find their way back to the foyer.

"Calm yourselves, Ladies!" Dr. Harris' voice commanded over the din. "I shall reverse the invocation presently and Mrs. Patterson will light additional sconces."

His announcement did little to sooth the upset of the seance attendees, but Adele did her best to move from chair to chair to reiterate the safety of the scene even as her hands and voice trembled.

"Spirits of the great beyond," The doctor's voice mingled with the rest. "I entrust you now back to the realm from which you came. Your presence is no longer welcome here!" The table rattled louder, crashing down upon the flooring as though being lifted and dropped. Mrs. Patterson managed to light an additional candle at the side of the room.

"To the entities present here, you are not welcome, and I command you back to your realm!"

The crashing softened back to a rattle as another candle came to life. The glow illuminated the group of women, huddled together near a side table, as well as the candelabra, which had fallen to the floor. Mrs. Patterson retrieved it and set to work re-igniting the tapers.

"I say again," Dr. Harris bellowed. "You are commanded to return from whence you came! I banish you hence and seal the portal with the cleansing certainty of my esoteric power!"

The rattling stopped and the room illuminated with the added effort of the candelabra to reveal Mrs. Barnes in a dead faint in her chair. Concern for their companion overtook the ladies' need to escape now that the direct threat seemed to have vanished. Mrs. Patterson hastened past Dr. Harris, who slumped wearily in his chair, and administered smelling salts. Adele focused on ushering the women toward the dining room, where they might ease their nerves with light refreshments.

Upon her return, Mrs. Barnes appeared far more alert and Mrs. Patterson patted her on the hand.

"Are the ladies well situated?" her employer asked, looking up as she drew near.

"Yes, they're all feeling much better now and are reviewing the experience with much enthusiasm now that it's over."

Mrs. Patterson returned her attention to Mrs. Barnes.

"Are you well enough to join them? Some tea with a fortifying dose of brandy will have you right as rain."

"I think that would be just the thing, Mrs. Patterson," Mrs. Barnes responded with a small nod of her head. "May I take your arm?"

"Yes, of course." Mrs. Patterson assisted Mrs. Barnes to rise, and the two women proceeded slowly toward the dining room. Adele made to follow, but Dr. Harris called her back.

"Mrs. Monroe, could you stay a moment longer? I'm sure Mrs. Patterson has the ladies well in hand and I fear I may yet need your assistance."

She turned back to the doctor, still slumped in his chair, and rushed to his side.

~

"Avery, are you quite well? How draining this entire evening must have been for you!" Adele clasped her hands, guilt rising at not having taken proper note of Dr. Harris' fatigue earlier. To her amazement, however, the moment she came within arm's reach, he hooked her about the waist and tugged her onto his lap, all signs of weariness vanishing as his lips curved to reveal a glorious white smile.

An instant later those lips pressed against hers in an insistent and passionate kiss which left her breathless with confusion. Realizing the shift in atmosphere, she considered providing a more enthusiastic response, but before she settled on a course of action the kiss came to an abrupt end, and Avery set her back on her feet.

"You were brilliant, my pet, just brilliant!" he patted her hip and she blushed, glancing toward the door.

"But I didn't do anything," she asserted, wondering what part of the evening he referenced.

"You gave the most genuine performance of shock and amazement!" he clarified. "Exactly what we needed to inspire feeling in our patrons."

She blinked at him. "I assure you it was no performance."

He furrowed his brow and observed her as though to ascertain the level of truth in her statement, then grinned at her as he rose from the chair.

"Even better, you have a true gift of sight in that case, you are a mover between the worlds. I knew it from the moment I laid eyes on you."

"Really?" How his compliments always managed to elicit surprise she couldn't say. She would have thought by now she'd grown accustomed to them. That she communed with spirits was true, but only one spirit, and Avery had no way of knowing that. His assertion therefore felt a bit misplaced.

"Yes, of course. Can you imagine the good work we will do together?" He leaned down to pick up the brass bell and set it on the table, following suit with the ear trumpet. "Tell me you've decided to tour with me when I leave here, do tell me."

Her shoulders sank. "Avery, I've already told you I can't possibly leave my children."

Losing all indication of joviality, he crossed his arms in front of him and glared. "A paltry excuse, I'm sure a boarding school would suit them quite well. Truly, I'm disappointed in you, Adele."

Adele gave a small gasp. "Disappointed? But you just said—"

"You have a grand spiritual calling," he lamented, throwing his hands up in the air for emphasis. "I'm sure you felt it tonight. How can you ignore it?"

In point of fact, she was not at all convinced she felt anything spiritually grand. She'd been just as frightened and uncertain as the rest of the women at the seance. Why, if Captain Daniels had attempted any such activity during her initial stay at the house, he could have easily secured her abandonment of it.

Her mind wandered back to the voice she reminded herself she no longer cared to hear. She wanted to race home and ask the captain if all spirits behaved so boorishly. He must be capable of it himself if the reports of how many potential renters he chased away were true, but that caused her to wonder why he behaved differently with her and allowed her to stay. Or perhaps there actually were other unfriendly entities wandering the universe intent on causing mischief.

Dr. Harris awaited her response with expectant eyes and a boyish, sullen expression. "I assure you, I'm not ignoring anything, but I must question the wisdom in such a large adjustment to my life."

"My pet, you must have more faith in the omnipotent divine! Do not question the how. Strike out on this course, move heaven and earth to make it so." He punctuated his statement with a gesture similar to those made when rooting on a favorite sports team.

Oh, how Adele wished she could ask the captain's advice, though she already knew what it would be. He would not approve of such rash behavior, whether it pertained to Dr. Harris or anyone else. She'd written his thoughts and contemplations often enough in the course of taking down the more adventurous portions of his stories to understand he'd always used reason to guide his decisions and set the welfare of his crew above his own. She might not have a ship and crew, but were a home and family not nearly the same?

And yet there was something so simplistically tempting in such a worldview as Dr. Harris'. To adopt a devil-may-care attitude just once and sail into the world as a free spirit. Such a thought provoked a rush of excitement. Another image of her children populated her thoughts and she sighed. Sometimes dreams were the only appropriate space for such flights of fancy. A sharp tell-tale pain stabbed at her heart. "I'm sorry, Avery, I just don't believe—"

"Was my adoration of you not sufficiently conveyed just now?" he argued, gesturing toward the seat he'd recently abandoned. "Surely you know how deeply I care for you. You are the other half of my soul," he clasped his palms over his heart. "We cannot deny the insistence of both the natural and supernatural worlds by remaining apart." He clasped her by the shoulders and stepped in close to her, disrupting the rational sequence of her thoughts. She took a step back.

"I…" She wrung her hands, needing an escape from this evening and all her conflicting thoughts.

An angry storm accumulated in his eyes and his features hardened. "You have wounded me beyond measure, Adele, truly."

She continued to search for words to appease him, but before her mind could land on any He stormed by her, exiting the room without a backward glance.

How ironic the captain insisted she focus on establishing relationships in the human world. As far as she could tell, her only talent lay in driving away any potential male acquaintance whether human or spectral. She sank down onto the chair Dr. Harris had vacated, folded her arms in front of her on the table, and rested her weary head atop them. She allowed herself a brief cry, diligently trying not to wish the captain would intrude upon her with the order to "belay that!"

CHAPTER 11

By the date of the next lecture, a mere day before the farewell breakfast, Adele assured herself she'd come up with a reasonable alternative to offer Dr. Harris. She understood his enjoyment of travel and shared an enthusiasm for it despite never gaining the opportunity to do so herself. But when they married, his proposal of which she felt certain lingered only on finding a mutually beneficial solution to this debate, he might consider establishing a single city from which to work and teach. Theosophy and his lectures surely garnered enough interest that with a bit of additional marketing his enthusiasts might be persuaded to come to him rather than he always to them.

If he must travel, perhaps a reduced schedule or one which accommodated the children's holiday schedule. She nodded to herself. Yes, they had both been too influenced by current patterns. When looked at objectively, a solution must present itself.

"Adira," the captain's voice startled her after his prolonged absence, halting her reach for the door.

"You've chosen a poor time to return," she remarked after taking a breath to calm her fluttering heart. "I'm on my way out, I have work."

"I know. And I also know what you're planning to discuss with Dr. Harris."

Her temper flared. "So, you've returned only to invade and judge my thoughts, then denounce me for them? I don't comprehend how you can in good conscience consider yourself a gentleman, Captain."

"It is an unforgivable intrusion made with noble intention. I'm concerned about you and worry you are about to make a detrimental decision."

"Because it runs counter to what you want."

"Because you are being deceived."

"That again. Captain, I contend it is your own jealousy and dislike of Dr. Harris which compels you to maintain this opinion. What proof have you to offer?"

"The seance."

"The seance?" she huffed. "What do you know about that? You refused to even entertain the thought of attending. I recall I made the offer."

"You did. But did you honestly believe I would let you attend such an event unescorted and without protection?"

She hesitated. The air in the parlor had seemed heavy in the way her room did now, but she dismissed it as an effect of all the drapes and doors being shut, along with the overabundant use of candles. "If you were at the seance, why did you not offer some sort of assistance during the spectral commotion?"

The wind sighed through the eaves. "Because there was no spectral commotion, my dear, it was a show meant to enthrall, nothing more."

"But I saw it all myself!" she insisted. "Avery's hands were still upon Mrs. Barnes' when the bell rang."

"The bell he placed on the ground on the far side of the table where you wouldn't see him use his foot to ring it."

Her eyes widened. What a ridiculous... then again, she supposed it possible. She never looked at the floor during the seance, and the table's cloth draped to the ground. She recalled to mind other events of the seance. "The candles doused themselves."

"Did you see the flames go out?"

"Of course I—" She cut off her statement. She'd been looking about the room when the light dimmed. "No, I didn't."

"Neither did anyone else. The women in the room were all intent on seeking out phantoms in the rafters. Your Dr. Harris blew the candles out amid the distraction."

The fragile hold on certainty and conviction she'd

managed to create for herself began to weaken. "And what about the table? Are you going to tell me it didn't rattle and jump?"

"No, it did rattle, but not of its own volition. Harris caused the motion with his knees."

A cloud of confusion descended on her thoughts and the plans so clear only a few minutes earlier. "So, there was never a ghost. And now poor Mrs. Barnes believes she communicated with her nephew!"

"No other ghost, no. And you need never perform a seance to compel my presence, Adira."

This was all too confusing, the captain's words and tone too effective in manipulating her heart. No, she would not allow it. She would make her own decision and her own judgments. What the captain claimed might be plausible but lacked any evidence beyond his assertion. "I will come to my own conclusions, Captain. Now if you will excuse me, I must be off to today's lecture."

"He's keeping secrets from you, Adira," the captain insisted as she reached again for the door.

"What sort of secrets?"

"I'm not certain yet, I only know that he is." The captain's voice took on a tinge of irritation.

"You make a poor case, Captain."

"I know, dammit, but it's not something I can readily explain."

"A good number of things exist you can't seem to explain. Perhaps you ought to abandon the attempt and leave me be." She reached for the door and turned the knob, but as she opened it, it flew shut again with a slam, the knob pulled from her hand. She gasped, staring at the door.

"Forgive me, I forgot myself, I..."

The captain's tone wrenched Adele's insides and she could muster no continued argument or anger. "Why are you so adamant Avery is deceiving me? Is it not possible he might be sincere in his feelings?" Tears stung her eyes. The captain's obsessive intent to dismantle Avery's character ignored the fact her own worth hung in the balance.

"My dear, you are so innocent and trusting and..." His words drifted away but she waited. "It's similar to... a shift in the atmosphere, like what you feel when I am present."

"What is?"

"This concern of mine. Not about Harris himself, from the start that has been what humans term a gut feeling, an inherent distaste for an untrustworthy rat. Call it jealousy if it appeases you. But I would not have reasserted myself on that old argument. Something else has entered the sphere of your being and I have no desire to see you harmed."

"Why would I be harmed? What is this shift?"

"I don't know. A person, but I don't know who. Someone is thinking of Harris and is not pleased by the thought. They are moving toward him, and whatever their intent, I prefer you to be far from him when they meet."

"Captain," Adele began after long moments mulling over his words. "I cannot allow you to dictate my life. I have never been prone to premonitions; therefore, I must continue on as I would without you here. I must attend to my responsibilities and find my own truths. I'm leaving now and will not entertain any further argument from you. Good day." She reached for the doorknob, hastening her movements in her desire not to show hesitation.

The knob turned and the door opened without issue. She hurried down the hall and stairs, pausing only long enough to bid farewell to Bessie and the children before leaving. The captain refrained from objection, though the prickling at her neck followed her through the house and out to the road, finally fading as the distance between her and the house lengthened.

~

Town Hall sat askew of the town it was meant to provide service to, not in the common center as most did but off to the inland side. Up to now no one objected, the entirety of the town nestled close enough together to make the trek to the hall negligible. In addition, accepting and converting the old barn for the purpose saved the town inhabitants a considerable sum at the time it was offered, negating the few objections made. The building witnessed few major assemblies and, therefore, was made available for event rentals. Today's lecture qualified for use of the space, as the participants outnumbered the available seating in Mrs. Patterson's home.

Adele arrived somewhat shaken, unnerved by the captain's words despite her parting recitation. Initially, she viewed every person who entered the hall with suspicion, wondering if they might be the person the captain alluded to. Eventually, due in large part to the increase in preoccupation related to small throngs of audience members arriving, Adele loosened her grip on those fears. She'd grown accustomed to her duties and fell easily into the routine of manning the registration table.

Given the time requirements for rental, Mrs. Patterson opted to divide the day's activities between free lecture reviews provided by herself, followed by the paid lecture Dr. Harris would present. A wall separated the front portion of the hall from the main section, creating an anteroom and ensuring the entrance and exit of attendees created minimal interruption for those in the main seating area. Adele's job was to collect registrations, respond to general questions, maintain the refreshments table on the opposite side of the room, and direct guests to it.

About mid-afternoon, long after Adele forgot about the captain's words, a woman walked into the hall, looking about as though lost.

"May I help you, ma'am?" She offered with a smile. The woman had a kind face, prettily plump and framed by golden ringlets. Only the small lines near the corners of her eyes and one or two beginning to show at the edges of her mouth indicated she might not be in the prime glow of youth but closer to Adele's own age. Her well-tailored attire suggested she came from a well-funded home, despite a skirt and jacket wrinkled from travel.

"Oh, perhaps," she returned Adele's smile. "Is this the location for the presentation on *Planetary Chains of the Cosmos* by the Theosophical Society?" Her eyebrows rose expectantly.

"It is, but I'm afraid the presentation won't begin for some time yet, are you on the guest roster?" Adele reached for the roster in question.

"No," the woman held up a gloved hand to stall her. "I don't actually mean to stay for the presentation, I'm here to speak to Dr. Harris."

An unfamiliar emotion bubbled up to Adele's throat. She couldn't say what it was, but it tasted sour and altered her view of the woman in front of her. The smile no longer shone with warmth, the eyes ceased to sparkle. Yes, Adele realized, this woman was far more drab than she'd initially thought. And perhaps the cloth of her dress wasn't quite so fine after all. "Oh, well, I'm afraid he hasn't arrived yet, did you have an appointment with him?"

"No, I find it generally easier to catch him without one."

Adele narrowed her eyes and pursed her lips. "Ah, well, I don't know that he'll have time, but if you let me know your name, I'd be happy to let him know when he gets here. I can't guarantee how long it will be, but if you'd like to wait, you're welcome to some refreshments." She directed the woman toward the table on the opposite end of the room.

"Thank you," the woman beamed. "That would be wonderful. You may tell him his wife, Cynthia Harris, is here to see him." She nodded, turning her attention to the cups and punch bowl.

A heaviness came over Adele, causing her head to swim. She swayed on her feet and might have crumpled altogether but some grace of circumstance propped her steady again on her feet. She blinked at the woman, Mrs. Harris, who had taken up prattling at her once she'd chosen a sandwich offering and turned her back on the refreshments.

"I don't usually bother him at these events, he gets very upset about it, but it's really quite urgent. Our eldest son has taken ill, and he hasn't responded to any of my wires. I decided I had to come out myself as the poor boy has been wailing for him inconsolably. Have you any children Mrs... Oh, dear, how remiss of me, I haven't even asked your name, and here you've been so helpful." She sent Adele a glowing smile.

"Mrs. Monroe," Adele whispered, clearing her throat before continuing. "Yes, a son and a daughter." The words formed, though she knew not how given the constriction in her throat and having almost no awareness of consciously forming them.

"Then you understand, I'm sure. Oh, how it tears at a mother's heart…"

"Cynthia!" Avery's voice resounded from the entryway, offering no hint of pleasant surprise.

Both women looked up to see a red-faced Dr. Harris glaring in their direction, though it appeared he aimed his displeasure at Cynthia. He focused so much vehemence in her direction, Adele wondered if he'd taken note of her at all. Cynthia, unperturbed by her husband's show of anger, set down her cup and plate to march swiftly in his direction. "Avery, dear, you haven't written, and little Avery is so despondent without you!"

"What are you doing here?" he growled through clenched teeth, taking her by the elbow and all but dragging her from the hall.

A wave of dizziness overtook Adele, but again some unexpected strength steadied her. The momentary reprieve opened the gates to a confusion bordering on madness. Married? She ran back to the reception table, grabbing blindly for her belongings. She ought to seek out Mrs. Patterson, complain of feeling unwell and insist on returning home, but she feared she hadn't the strength for such politeness. Stumbling to the door and down the steps, sparing only one glance off to the side where heightened voices indicated an argument in progress.

Dr. Harris stood opposite his wife near an outcropping of trees, gesturing wildly. Hints of his voice floated along the breeze, though they were too far for any snippets to be heard clearly. Cynthia argued in return, though sadness, rather than anger, highlighted her sentiments, as evidenced by the handkerchief she clutched to her cheek at the ready to maneuver toward either eyes or nose.

A small, strangled expression of pain escaped Adele as she forced herself to concentrate on the road in front of her. She returned home as swiftly as she could manage, thankful she needn't pass directly through town along her way. How she managed it remained a mystery, the weight of the world seemed to drag down her every step.

Every tree and bush reached out sharp claws to dig into her skirts. Stumbling more than once along the journey, her eyes filled with tears until her vision blurred so significantly, she relied on muscle memory alone to guide her. By the time she reached her home and stumbled her way past a startled Bessie to reach the sanctuary of her room, she was convinced it had to have been divine intervention that carried her home.

CHAPTER 12

"No, not divine," she croaked to herself at some point later when her tears had eased and breathing settled. "You're here, aren't you?"

"Yes," the captain responded.

"You were at the hall too, weren't you?" She recalled her lightheadedness, the willingness of her mind to faint away from the scene tearing at her heart. She might like to think it was her own strength of will that kept her standing, but she knew better.

"Yes."

"Are you the reason she appeared at the hall? Did you incite her to come here?" Her tear-roughened voice sounded petty to her ears, but she hadn't the strength to care. She'd cried half the evening away. Bessie knocked once to tell her she'd left a tray by the door, and the deep orange glow of the sun's descent lamented the hour.

"No, I couldn't have thrown the truth at you in that way, you may think me generally heartless, but I wouldn't have been that cruel." His voice was soft but tinged with a mild anger. To whom he directed that anger, she couldn't tell.

"You must think me every sort of a fool and a ninny," She buried her head in her pillow once more, a self-deprecating moan wrenching from her throat in lieu of the tears her worn and aching eyes failed to produce.

"No," he soothed. "Your only fault is a heart too generous and I'm about to lose whatever corner of it I might have earned. Say you'll forgive me, Adele."

"Forgive you for what?" She sniffed, laying still atop her bed and holding her breath, fearful of his next words.

"This is my fault. I should have continued to dissuade you, done more to prevent his attentions toward you. But you were so adamant!" he growled, though the sound of displeasure managed to circle back to himself rather than her. "I thought I'd leave off for a bit, let you learn a lesson and intervene before he caused too much damage to your heart, but then..."

She sat up, staring into the dim room. "Then what?"

"When you spoke of the seance. Perhaps I heard more than you intended in the words, but I thought you'd developed too great of an attachment to the otherworldly. Also my doing, blast it! I convinced myself you needed some incentive to rejoin the living."

"So, you allowed me to think a married man was courting me?" her heart lurched.

"No! Yes. Not deliberately! I had no more knowledge of that than you."

"How could that be?" Adele argued in exasperation. "You seem to always know everything about everyone. Isn't that a benefit of the afterlife?"

"I can only know the thoughts of those among whom I circulate. He never thought of her, not once. It wasn't until she journeyed here and was close enough to emit her thoughts that I suspected something."

"And I dismissed your warning." She closed her eyes, letting her chin drop to her chest.

"I'm so sorry, Adele, I've apparently learned nothing for all my talk of universal knowing in the afterlife. No wonder I remained attached to this house, too stubborn to remit my self-important human tendencies."

The air rippled with the captain's seething self-anger.

"But..." Adele's teetering mind searched for a thread to hold to, still unwilling to comprehend how completely wrong she'd been. "You may have allowed the events to unfold, but you couldn't have put the feeling into his heart. He said he loved me. He said his soul recognized mine!"

"He lied."

"Must you always be so blunt, Captain?" Her heart twisted in her chest, the muscles in her face twisting again into a grimace of anguish. "He promised to show me the world, to teach me so many things I don't know…"

"Adele…"

"He kissed me! How could he have kissed me that way if he didn't love me, it's not possible!"

When next the captain spoke, his words were soft and comforting. "What did you feel when he kissed you?"

Her cheeks flared at the intimacy, and impertinence, of the question. Part of her wanted to shrink away, indulge in her sorrow, but another part wished he were tangible so she could fold herself into his arms and let him block out the world. The question confused her. Obviously she felt love, what other response was there when a man kissed you?

"I felt… I felt the way I did when my husband kissed me."

"Then you didn't feel what you were meant to. You didn't feel love."

"Who are you to tell me that?" She straightened, anger flaring once again. "I suppose you're going to have a fine laugh now at my foolishness in believing his talk about souls and soul mates. Twin flames and the like."

"No, that was true." His statement held a strength of conviction which left no room for argument, causing Adele to press her lips together when she would otherwise have responded.

"Remember," he continued. "He has the kernel of

truth but not the incentive to actually strive toward a better understanding of it." He paused, and Adele imagined him as she'd seen him in her dream that first night, pacing in front of the fireplace and chewing on his pipe. Perhaps, if she could see him, he would be slightly hunched, in the manner of a man attempting to reason out a dilemma.

"Souls," he resumed, "do recognize each other. We are all part and parcel of each other and sometimes two, or more, will form an attachment which lasts through many incarnations. But when two souls of intimate connection recognize each other, they both feel it. When one reaches for the other there is an immediate physiological response, it's like... damnation, there are no proper words!"

"Of course not," Adele snorted, weary from her emotional extremes. "The words never exist when they're important do they? You'll never explain anything to me any better than Dr. Harris meant to, will you? And where am I to stand in all of this? A misfit in the physical world and rejected by the spiritual, more confused now than I was before I came here. Oh, I wish I'd never seen this wretched house!" She slumped down on the bed once again, gathering up her pillow and burying her face in it.

"Adele—"

"Go away!" she shouted into the pillow. "Go away and leave me be. I don't want anything else to do with you!

Not with ghosts, not with Dr. Harris and Theosophy, none of it! If I'm meant for nothing more than existence, I don't want any more interruptions to it. Let me get through it in peace!"

He didn't respond, but neither did he leave her. An unseen shimmer remained in the air, a hint of tobacco smoke so faint one would question having smelled it. Adele didn't leave her room, or even move from her bed. She lay there, still fully dressed, tossing from one side to the other, alternating between contemplation and renewed tears. The sun sank beneath the horizon as she stared up to the ceiling for advice. The sky shrugged into its diamond-studded midnight robe, still she despaired of sleep. Not until several hours after the final ringing of the clock downstairs did her mind give up its hold and allow her to sink into restful oblivion.

∾

A BLANKET of darkness enveloped the room when Adele next opened her eyes. An odd quality hung in the air, something simultaneously familiar and strange. She sat up and swung her legs over the side of the bed. Unusually heavy legs, though she attributed this to the harried exit she'd made from town hall yesterday.

Her room swayed before her eyes. The floor and walls, hazy in the darkness, were alluded to but somehow unseen. Her eyes wandered to a warm glow at the far end of the room by the fireplace. Not the fireplace itself, but a lamp on the table. Squinting, she rose and approached that corner, her bed and the rest of the room behind her swallowed by the dark as she moved in frustratingly slow steps.

She halted in front of the table, staring at the lamp. A beautiful lamp, shaded by an intricate stained glass and crystal creation. It gave off a deep amber radiance which existed as a protracted halo illuminating only itself and the table it sat on. Why did she feel confusion?

"It's not your lamp," The Captain informed her.

She turned to face the armchair. Vacant when she'd passed by a mere moment before, the captain now occupied the space, pipe in hand.

"It's not?" she asked.

"No, it was a favorite piece of mine, bought in France in younger days. Gaudy, don't you think? I thought it elegant at the time."

She turned her head to look at the piece again, only succeeding for an instant before whipping her attention back to him. "Captain!"

"My name is Gregory, Madam, I do wish you would learn to use it."

"I can see you!"

"Indeed."

"But how?"

"Come now, my dear, you know the answer to that."

"I'm dreaming," she whispered, looking about the room again and realizing it had vanished into darkness around them, only the small corner they occupied remained. A sudden fear of the unknown gripped her, seizing her heart and sending sparks flying through her, reminding her of the ineffectual heaviness of her limbs.

"Steady now," the captain rose, reaching for her arm as he set his pipe on the table beside the lamp.

An instant calm engulfed her, though she felt no press of his hand against her, only a heavy warmth hugging her. He stood before her, observant.

"But how is it I know I'm dreaming?" She wondered aloud and swayed. The movement not so much a movement of her body as a swaying of the room about her. She comprehended she stood, yet she felt herself lying down, her body a weight pressing into the mattress of her bed. She wanted to turn her head to look for the bed, but couldn't manage it.

"A simple lucid dream. A state of existence somewhere between earthly and divine. You sail these waters often enough in your sleep, you simply don't remember."

"Will I forget this?"

"Perhaps, though it's unlikely. Remembered dreams are most often those experienced in this state which are interrupted."

"Why would my dream be interrupted?"

"Because it is not only your spirit self which experiences."

"I don't understand."

"You will." He gazed at her, seeming to see something far beyond whatever image she cast in this strange dream time.

For her part, Adele didn't mind staring back. Something in those shimmering blue eyes set her heart to racing. She took in a sighing breath, again feeling herself in two places at once and tamping down the uneasiness that brought with it. "Why are you here? Have I conjured you into my dreams after telling you to leave me be?"

He smiled, tiny lines appearing at the corners of his eyes and compelling her to lean in closer to him.

What a frustratingly strange thing, this wakeful dreaming. It showed her only segments of images. The captain's face smiling down at her, the edge of his arm and side as she leaned in toward him, but never the feeling of coming into contact with him.

"Alas," he responded, the echo of his voice beside her ear. "I must beg your forgiveness yet again. You did not summon me here, I invaded your thoughts of my own volition."

"Why?"

"Because I could not leave things as they were." He shifted, appearing square in front of her again. "I thought perhaps in this manner I could show you something of what I so poorly explained in our argument."

"I don't see how it would be easier, if you didn't have the words then, why would you have them now?"

"I don't need them now. We are essentially both in spirit form. We can greet each other on equal ground."

Mention of the ground brought to Adele the realization she felt no floor beneath her, setting off another flare of panic before the captain's reassuring warmth swaddled her again.

"If you frighten yourself awake," he chastised gently, "I won't succeed in my endeavor. Take a breath."

She felt the movement in her other self and focused on the man in front of her. "Greet each other?" she asked, grasping at a distraction which might keep her in her dream.

"Yes. One soul reaching for the other, there is a sense of deep knowing when they meet, a kinship. Will you allow me to show you?"

She nodded.

He held out his hands to her and she slid her palms over his. A current of something wonderful washed through her and she shut her eyes. The forgotten innocent joy of childhood, the first surge of feeling when one finds the person they've been thinking of has also been thinking of them. The electric prickling of awareness. Her earthly body shivered and she tightened her grip. The feeling hinted at unseen pleasures, hidden wonders, and she allowed her muscles to relax, compelled her dream forward. She breathed in deeply, letting out a sigh.

Captain Daniels pulled away from her, shocking her out of the moment, but thankfully not out of the dream.

When she opened her eyes, he wore a look of confusion. The scene around them had changed. They stood together on a beach near the cliffs. The captain stared at her, his expression beginning to cause her some fright.

"What's wrong?" she asked.

"I think..." he ducked his chin. "I may have been wrong in what I thought I could convey. I should let you rest." He turned from her, and she felt the pull of the waking world as her other self turned in bed.

A sensation of dizzying emptiness followed, a void enlarging with each heartbeat. The fear of her dreaming mind returned, the fear of losing this closeness with the soul who had become so dear to her. She felt the tightening of something about her heart, an unseen securement which would snap if the captain drifted too far.

"Captain, wait!" she reached out to him, took hold of his arm, and embraced him when he turned. It wasn't an embrace in the way she knew it while awake, but an all-consuming warmth. A steadiness of being. When he leaned his head against hers a heaviness overtook her senses and her surroundings melted away yet again, re-forming as a narrow opening in the cliffside.

Her heart beat frantically and her breath heightened. "Captain?"

"I'm here with you," his voice enveloped her, warmth washing over her. She stepped into the entrance. A tunnel opened in front of her, at first too dark to navigate. She set her palm against the wall to guide her. The wall illumined with a burst of golden shimmer, and she snatched her hand back.

"Don't shy away," the captain's whisper sounded at her ear. A trail of subdued heat worked its way down from her shoulder to her hand, compelling it back to the wall. The otherworldly light returned, silver shot through with gold. A stabilizing presence at her back, and another tendril of heat snaking over her hip and around to coil at her belly, a comforting pressure.

She took a step forward, the light shooting off into the distance and returning, compelling her to follow. With each step, she lost herself a bit more in the dream, racing into an unknown. Her form shimmered with the guiding glow pulsing above and around her until she lost her cognizance of it completely and existed only as a being intent on finding the hidden source of those lights.

Somewhere in the far recesses of her knowing, her earthly body took on more rapid breathing, heart beating fiercely to maintain her unseen motion. Muscles twitched in confusion, wanting to dictate movement of her limbs but unable to.

The captain never left her, his energetic presence surrounding her, then receding, merging with her and separating. In those moments they came together her whole being trembled with the pleasure of it. Tension built in her earthly self, a tension born of knowing two souls cannot truly merge when confined to earthly forms. She squirmed in her restless dreaming.

The dream offered freedom. An ethereal dance of two souls swirling through and around each other. She wanted to laugh but was still tied too tightly to her breathless body. She soared through the tunnel, heart aching in frustration. This must lead to a place she could find the captain and stay with him always, create one whole from two incomplete pieces.

A rushing took up in her ears, her earthly pulse sending blood racing through the maze of its confinement, searching for release, stirring up her most basic desires. Rivulets of water trickled along the walls, reflecting the ever-increasing flashes of light. Her earthly self panted. The captain filled her senses, took hold of her and remained. Excitement circled her heart and darted out to her limbs, raced back and confronted him where he'd taken up residence in the innermost core of her, two opposing currents whirling around each other in a play for dominance which could only lead to crashing together and forming something altogether new.

The rush of water around her increased, the tunnel walls now continually assaulted by it and the pulses of light shortening in anticipation of a destination. She wrapped herself around the familiar warmth of the captain, a pinpoint of light in the distance burgeoning as they dashed to meet it. Everything seemed to converge at once. The rushing in her ears, the racing of her heart and her shallow breaths. A vibration rolled upward from the deepest part of her, breaking away from the confinement of the flesh as her spirit self tumbled through an opening and plummeted.

In an instant she was pulled harshly back through time and space to settle with a start into her still gasping mortal shell. In that moment when her dream world burst around her, her eyes shot open to stare at the ceiling above her as her muscles contracted and pulsed. The traitorous vibration lingered at her throat, and she realized she must have made some sound, jarring her and waking her from her dream. She inhaled, unable to alter position as her leaden limbs were not yet under the control of her newly wakened mind. Her heart raced in her chest and her head felt light. She trembled in place for what seemed an eternity before her senses began to settle.

She blinked at the room around her. The familiar room. Her heart still fluttered, but she felt solid enough now to shift to her side. "Gregory?"

"Yes?" the captain responded, his voice a strained rasp in her consciousness.

"That... that felt like a great deal more than kinship to me."

"Yes." He intoned, giving no hint to his thoughts on the matter.

"What then..." She searched for the words, deciding to begin again. "Would the meeting of soul mates be somehow amplified even greater than that?" She couldn't imagine such a thing, barely believing she'd survived this meeting. Her body was still aflame and only a heightened sense of timidity kept her from throwing off her covers now that she had the muscular capability to do so.

"No," he responded, the word infused with anguish. "It would feel just like that."

CHAPTER 13

*L*ate morning sun filtered through the French doors before Adele stirred from her slumber. Not surprising given the maelstrom of emotions the previous day, and night, provoked.

"Bessie poked her head in to check on you not long ago," the captain's voice informed her. "She'll call for the doctor if you don't go downstairs soon, but I hadn't the heart to wake you. You are quite angelic when you sleep, you know."

"Am I?" she stood, taking a moment to stretch her torso before making her way to the dressing table. The image reflected in the mirror smacked more of Medusa than Madonna, her hair a mangled explosion of misplaced pins and half-secured tresses. She frowned.

"Well, most nights anyway," the captain chuckled.

"How often do you leer at me while I sleep?"

"I respectfully decline to answer that question."

Adele began picking pins from her hair, digging her fingers through the mass in search of those lost in the abyss. Once pleased with her progress, she raked through her hair to disentangle the majority before attempting an attack with her brush. The process proved lengthy but provided her time to remember the events of her dreaming. After a time, the captain questioned her.

"What has you so pensive, my dear? The lines you're creating between your eyebrows will become permanent if you don't smooth them soon."

"A thought occurred to me."

"That bodes ill."

"Don't tease, I have a serious question."

"Very well, what do you wish to know?"

"Do you remember when you told me that time isn't linear?"

"Yes..." He drew out the word.

"And you asserted that reincarnation does happen."

"Yes..."

"If there are multiple concurrent dimensions, couldn't you—"

"I must insist you change tack immediately. Your present course will lead to folly."

At least his swift response, though not positive, indicated he either considered the thought himself or realized she would. "But why? If it's not possible for a soul to return to earth at a time which may coincide with the life they previously lead, then your earlier argument about non-linear reincarnation is void, isn't it?"

"It's not a matter of it being impossible, my dear, it simply isn't done."

"What about the idea of a doppelganger? Is an instance of meeting someone in your lifetime who looks exactly like you some completely different phenomenon?"

Silence stretched to just shy of snapping. "It ought not to be done."

"Why not?"

"The incarnated soul, once born into the earthly plane becomes subject to the influences of that reality. The essence of the soul would be the same, but it wouldn't be a complete match."

"But wouldn't it be enough?"

"Not necessarily. Additionally, the reincarnated soul would have no memory of the reason for the return to earth, leaving him or her essentially drifting rudderless. It's far too great of a risk, Adira."

"You don't believe we are meant for each other, then." She attempted not to sound like a disappointed child. "What was the purpose of your influencing my dream if I still don't understand?"

"You do understand." He murmured. "I should not have interfered but didn't realize, or rather, hadn't acknowledged..."

"What?" She insisted when his words faded.

"I cannot be without you and will not leave you unless you wish it. "But the best option," he hastened to add, "if you wish us to be on equal footing is to wait until the end of your current lifetime."

"But that could be sixty years or more from now!"

"Hopefully, yes. Reincarnation is a choice, Adira, I will happily wait for you."

"But what if—"

"Stop talking," he snapped, his voice taking on its familiar commanding mantle.

"How very like a man to dictate behavior."

"Adele, you must keep quiet."

"No, I tell you, I won't. Haven't you been telling me to be assertive and independent? All fine fluff I suppose—"

"Now is not the time to heed my advice. Please."

"It can work, I'm sure it can. If it is the inner being of a person we are meant to adhere ourselves to in love, then—"

She turned in her seat, preparing to rise, but halted in her movements. The glow of hope and excitement newly realized drained into the floorboards with a heaviness that pulled at her eyes and jaw, widening them into a silent show of terror.

Her mother-in-law stood in the doorway, one lace-gloved hand still resting atop the knob, the other pressing a handkerchief to the corner of her nose as her eyes tested various shapes as though unsure which emotion to settle on. "I knew it. I just knew it," she stated with a shake of her head. "Henry told such fanciful tales during his visit about an imaginary sea captain friend—"

"A sea captain?" Adele narrowly avoided spinning around in search of the captain. The gesture wasn't necessary in any case. A dull groan running through her thoughts confirmed his guilt.

"And dreams of far-off places," the elder Mrs. Monroe continued, ignoring her question. "I dismissed it at first as boyish imagination, but his age is certainly outside the realm of such silly preoccupation. I became so concerned I decided I must make the trip out immediately to consult with you about it, this minuscule town is obviously not providing enough intellectual stimulation for the boy. Now I see I should be more concerned about you!" her expression took on a hint of horror.

Adele cleared her throat. "I'm sure my behavior must appear rather strange, mother. But I am simply working through my thoughts. "Verbalization really is the best way to do so."

"Thoughts about reincarnation? Heavens, had I known when I left here last you would be working for such a blasphemous cause as a Theosophical Society! They've muddled your head, dear girl!"

"How did—"

"I wrote to Mrs. Patterson to inquire. How shameful of you to have me believe you were employed in some respectable position in the mayor's home. I'm surprised the man is still in office if he allows his wife to associate with such questionable sorts! Yet another black mark against this horrid little fisherman's village!"

"I assure you I am mentally sound, mother, and this town—"

"You try to tell me this after Bessie informed me you weren't feeling well and hadn't come down yet, and looking for all the world as though you've slept in your clothes!"

Adele's palms ran instinctively down the seams of her dress before she managed to halt them.

"And what's more," her mother-in-law continued, "you looked as though you truly *believed* you were in conversation with someone!"

"How can that be, mother?" Adele attempted a strained laugh. "You can see as well as I there's no one here. You mustn't worry over me, I'm perfectly sound."

The woman shook her head, crocodile tears now floating in her red-rimmed eyes. "To think what this is doing to my poor grandchildren..."

"But mother, surely you don't believe—"

"There's no help for it." She straightened her posture in a show of uncharacteristic conviction. "Adele, I'm going to keep the children with me."

"What? You can't do that!"

"It's in their best interests, dear. Now, my friend Mrs. Aimes is acquainted with a fine psychologist in Boston. If you would visit him and receive a clean bill of mental health, I would have no qualms sending the children back to you, though I fear I may never be of sound conscience regarding all of you again."

"But there's no need!" Adele tempered a screech. "I'm perfectly sound!" She took a step in her mother-in-law's direction, but the woman's eyes widened and she swiftly retreated. Adele followed her to the hall, but she'd taken on astounding speed in her movements, calling from the stairway, "I'll arrange for the children's travel and wire you the referral!"

The front door slammed in her wake before Adele reached the stairway landing.

"What an interfering old bat," the captain commented. "If she would—"

"You went back on your word!" Adele accused. "You promised not to leave the bedroom! And you lied about it to boot!"

"It's amazingly difficult to temper one's wanderings, especially within one's own home."

"Does that change the fact?"

"No, though in my defense you recall your primary objective in keeping me away from your children was to prevent frightening them and, you see, no such fright occurred."

She clasped her hands together to prevent them reaching for the nearest decor and hurling it at the wall. Breathing deeply, she endeavored to calm her frantic thoughts long enough to apply reason to her dilemma. She marched back to her room, thoughts racing. This could go very badly. She needed to reassert herself in her mother-in-law's good graces.

"You're not going to let that woman cow you, are you?" the captain questioned. "They are your children."

"Yes, but my mother and sister-in-law are women with far more influence than I, and if I force them to legal action and the authorities ask Henry about his statements?"

A sigh. "He's an honest lad, he'll tell the truth."

"Exactly. No, I must go to Boston to prove my sanity, though I'm beginning to doubt it myself."

~

Within the week, Adele stood outside a drab, multi-storied brick building, noting the severity of the rusting iron fence which extended out from the building's side to enclose an extended wing and garden grounds.

"The old barge sent you to a blasted asylum!" the captain fumed. "What's wrong with keeping an office in an office building? The man can't be reputable."

Adele reached for the chain-link bell pull to indicate her arrival. "Would you please refrain from commentary? You know I would have preferred you not accompany me at all." A blatant lie. She'd initially insisted the captain remain at Coral Cottage, but the nearer she ventured toward the location of her appointment the happier she was to have his company.

"I shall refrain from comment only if such commentary is not vitally necessary."

She sighed but supposed that would be the best response he'd offer. A bolt in the massive oak door receded from its post with a heavy thud, followed by a creak loud enough to rival any horror production as the portal swung open.

"Yes?" A pale-faced, white-clad attendant asked through the mask of a bland expression.

"I have an appointment to see Dr. Garrison. I'm Mrs. Monroe."

Without acknowledging the statement, the dismal specter tugged the door open a hair wider and indicated she should pass. Once she did so, he reversed the process, setting the bolt back into place before silently preceding Adele down the hall. She kept pace, desiring to avoid any accidental separation. Her footsteps clicked across the tiling, the sound echoing along surrounding surfaces and mingling with a collection of curious noises emanating from somewhere beyond the walls.

They came to a halt in front of a door adorned with a copper plaque declaring it the office of Dr. Garrison. Moments later, she'd been escorted in, made to sit in a chair across from a desk, and left to await the entrance of said doctor. The wait proved short.

"Good day, Mrs. Monroe," A white-haired man of indistinguishable years greeted her with the same enthusiasm as the door attendant. "I'm glad to see you. Your mother-in-law was adamant in her concern for you, and I must say she mentioned a few things that cause me concern as well." He sank heavily into his seat, flipping open a file folder and concentrating the whole of his attention on it.

"I'm here as a courtesy to my mother-in-law, Dr. Garrison," Adele responded. "But I assure you there is no reason for concern."

"That remains to be seen," he muttered." Now, to begin with, I'm told that after the death of your husband you moved into a home at quite a distance from your family?"

"The further from that lot the better." The captain growled, causing Adele to shift in her seat.

"I wouldn't call it quite a distance, it's not an inconvenient trip by rail."

"And what was your reason for the move?"

"I was unwilling to remain a burden on my husband's family and thought it best to create an independent household for myself and my children. It also provided us all more space for privacy and personal pursuits."

"Mmm," the doctor pursed his lips and scribbled onto a page in the folder. "Grief is a delicate matter, Mrs. Monroe, I've often seen widows of every age make rash decisions in their mourning, no longer privy to the stabilizing presence of a man."

"I don't believe my decision—"

"Your mother-in-law expressed a concern about how

you were able to afford your home, I understand your husband left you only a small annuity…"

"That's none of his damned business!"

"The house came at a good price due to the owner being absent and keen on a sale." Adele responded with a tight smile.

"An absentee owner. I imagine the place must have been dilapidated to fetch a sufficiently low price, perhaps not the best environment to bring children into?"

"What an idiotic old—"

"The house was in very good repair for the most part, it only wanted for a little—"

"Such places will often incite imaginative tales in the psyches of small children likely to be frightened by a sudden uprooting of the familiar."

"My children were delighted at the—"

"I understand your son began telling tales of ghosts in the house."

Adele clenched her teeth. "More of an imaginary friend, really. Boys are always a little wont to create tales of adventure, aren't they? The house was built by a sea captain, I'm sure he only meant to impress his new school friends."

More furious scribbling.

"Children aren't the only ones who might be negatively affected by sudden isolation, Mrs. Monroe. I understand you have taken to speaking to yourself, a habit your mother-in-law assures me you did not have previously."

"Why did she bother insisting you come here if the two of them have already psychoanalyzed you in detail amongst themselves?"

"I find that sorting out ideas verbally helps me to clarify them more rapidly. I did not indulge in this habit in my mother-in-law's home for fear of disturbing her."

"Mmm..." Dr. Garrison tapped his pencil on the folder. "Your mother-in-law also informed me you have taken employment outside the home, is this correct?"

"It is, though I'm not certain why you seem to view that negatively. It is quite common—"

"Terribly unfortunate what the instability of a home without a male lead might force a woman into, that cannot be contested. Might I ask what sort of employment you have taken up?"

"Careful, my dear."

"I work for a local social organization, assisting with files and events."

"Good."

"And the name of your employer?"

"Damn."

"Mrs. Patterson."

Dr. Garrison finally looked up from his file to spear her with a look of admonishment. "Would that by chance be the same Mrs. Patterson who has recently hosted a lecture tour by a so-called Dr. Harris?"

"Bilge rat! Your mother-in-law must have informed him, that Harris wouldn't be known here otherwise."

Adele deflated. "Yes."

"Good heavens, Mrs. Monroe, I am quite relieved you came in when you did." He set down his pencil, shut the file and rose, making his way toward a switch panel on the side wall. Pressing one of the buttons, he clasped his hands behind him and turned back to his desk. "You were obviously heading down a dangerous path. Your mother-in-law was quite right to recommend this office to you."

"What a self-righteous, pompous—"

"I'll have a room prepared for you at once in the ladies' ward."

"A room?"

A sudden gale took up outside, as evidenced by the violent swaying of tree branches outside the doctor's window.

"Yes, it is imperative that you remain here under strict supervision until I can adequately root out the sources of your mental confusion and see to your proper re-education."

"Mental confusion? I haven't got any—"

"Never fear, Mrs. Monroe, I have every confidence we have caught the trouble early enough that a full recovery can be achieved within a matter of weeks."

"Weeks?! I won't stay here for weeks on end!"

The doctor halted in his pacing toward his chair and fixed her with a glare. "Mrs. Monroe, you have no choice. Your mother-in-law has recommended you to my care and it is my professional stance that a recuperative stay is necessary to prevent any further degeneration of your mental state."

"But Doctor—"

A knock at the door sounded an instant before a middle-aged woman, somewhat stout and just as pale as everyone here seemed to be, entered.

"Nurse Davies," the doctor acknowledged. "Please escort Mrs. Monroe to the ladies' ward and help her to settle into a room."

CHAPTER 14

The room Nurse Davies ushered Adele into reeked of caustic chemical cleansers incapable of restoring the cracked, dingy tile to its original white. A brass-framed bed occupied one corner, its thin, sagging mattress mummified in threadbare white linen and an exceptionally rough-looking gray wool blanket. No other furniture occupied the narrow space. Although the draining nature of the day compelled her to sit, her mind would not yet allow it. Instead, she wandered to the small window set high enough in the wall to prevent effortless viewing of the gloomy day outside. On the other side of the bars, a tree's emaciated branches reached in agony toward rain-laden clouds. When had the seasons changed? A parched leaf caught in the wind and floated away.

How much had changed since this time last year, she

thought, and how much was yet to change. She let out a sigh as she sank down from her toes and released the windowsill to turn again into the void of her new room. Last year, she'd looked upon change as an emancipation. Now, it entombed her.

"Why do the living always fancy themselves so damned all-important?" The captain's voice boomed through Adele's thoughts louder than a foghorn. She scrunched her eyes shut and ducked her chin, willing her thoughts to remain hidden. They were difficult enough to consider and she doubted her ability to hold fast to them if the captain waged an argument against them.

Hopefully, his own self-important nature might distract his attention, at least for the span of his tirade. "No matter, we shall see you out of this brig and on your way home in time for the evening meal. Now, what you'll do—"

"I'll do nothing." She breathed, swallowing down the distaste which followed.

"I beg your pardon?"

"I'll do nothing. I suppose I always realized the risk I ran in conversing with you, the inherent misunderstanding should it ever become known."

"Madam, you shall not take on the weight of the world's ignorance. You are in the right, they are in the wrong, and we will get you out of here in no time whatsoever."

"It's what you warned me of, isn't it? I must not overstep the bounds between life and death. But I thought myself so much more mature, so enlightened."

"And that you are, you have a far greater understanding of the ways of the larger world than the common air-breather."

"No," she smiled. "I am every bit as childish. I became too comfortable, I began to... to imagine a life I had no right to, and you see the divine has broken the wings of my selfish flight of fancy."

She paused, holding her breath, but only silence answered her. Even so, the prickling at the nape of her neck, the heavy warmth she'd come to yearn for as surely as any human touch, wrapped her in the security of its embrace. She inhaled deeply, lingering. "You had the right of it. I am a living creature, I belong in a living world, and all my arguments and desires cannot change that. My only recourse now is to convince the doctor and my in-laws that I am every bit as mentally sound as they are. Repent my madness on bended knee and pray they return my children to me."

The warmth surrounding her shifted, the heaviness in the air expanding.

"And I am no more the wiser for my years in the afterlife. I suppose this is why I've been fated to remain wandering. Let it be known, Madam, you are not the only one who wished for a private place of residence between the worlds." The words gave way to silence, and when he spoke again his speech regained its former vigor. "Be that as it may, the present is as it is, and between the two of us we shall have your independence repaired as quickly as possible."

"No."

"What?"

"You must not try to aid or protect me. Don't you see? As long as you remain in my thoughts, I stand no chance of pretending otherwise."

"Lying is certainly not your strong point but, my dear, you cannot be suggesting—"

"You must leave." There. She said it. And because she'd steeled herself against the moment the tearing of her heart only caused her eyes to water and her anguish remained unvoiced.

"If you feel it would be best in aiding your cause, I will certainly stand watch at Coral Cottage, but you need only call to me—"

"You must leave me completely."

A wind hurtled by, sending the skeletal tree outside into convulsions. "The devil I must! You have no grounds for such a request, and Coral Cottage is as much my home as it ever was."

"Then I shall sell the place on my release and move."

Thunder rumbled across the darkened sky and a draft howled through a flue in the hall.

"I'm beginning to believe that quack's diagnosis of you," the captain growled. "What insanity has possessed you to such extremes of thought? You have no reason to sell and have often argued the perfection of the spot for you and your brats."

"And as long as I am conversant with you, I will know no peace. An air of doubt will always accompany me, my privacy will be forever lost, besieged by the prying eyes of my in-laws and the entire town no doubt once my current situation becomes known."

The air inside the small room sizzled and cracked. "Damn the town and your in-laws!"

"That tactic has not succeeded for me thus far, Captain. Which brings me back to my aforementioned point. So long as you are near, I cannot maintain my facade, as I cannot keep from speaking to you. You must abandon me completely."

A prolonged silence ensued, during which another broadside of thunder shook the building. Sharp droplets of rain pelted the window seeking entry, and the low baying in the hall elevated to a prolonged banshee's wail. Adele straightened her shoulders and tipped up her chin, prepared for the captain's squall.

The storm retreated with caution, leaving the stillness of time suspended. A deep chuckle, one she hadn't heard for some time, rolled over and through her.

"No," he whispered at her ear. "I dare not test my dear Adira, isn't that so? A competent captain does not plot a course into a storm. Damn this trick of time which kept you always a voyage away, a siren's song in the fog. Had I still a heart to give... Blast!"

A sudden rush of air traversed the room, and a chill ran through her, sucking the air from her lungs. Outside, the storm calmed as quickly as it had formed, the wind dying away and the sky lightening. Blinking, she realized her mind felt horribly clear, her ears miserably silent. Wrapping her arms about herself as her heart clenched in her chest, she sank onto the narrow, sterile bed. With what small reserve of breath was left her she managed, "Good-bye, Gregory," before allowing herself to indulge in weeping.

She wept for her circumstance, she wept for the loss of her children, but she wept all the harder knowing her captain's voice would no longer admonish her to end her weeping.

CHAPTER 15

"On the matter of hearing voices and speaking to yourself, you have vastly improved," Dr. Garrison conceded at the conclusion of Adele's most recent evaluation. Outside, winter lay in full regalia across the city, icy winds preventing anyone who could avoid it from disturbing the pristine white mantle. Adele's keepers afforded her little time to view the scene herself, but the cold made itself known through the shoddy seals around her window.

She slumped back against her chair, recognizing in the doctor's voice his preparation for a rebuttal of the positive statement. She'd assured herself in her first days at the facility that without the captain's distraction she could easily convince the doctor of her sanity and return home. That hadn't been the case. Nothing she said placated the man. Each day became more of a chore to overcome. And the captain remained away.

"But I still have a few concerns about your views related to domesticity." The doctor continued.

Of course. He always had a few more concerns and Adele struggled to search for and create responses she hoped would match his opinions. She barely suppressed a snort. How had she ever believed the medical field relied on objective reason. Within a medical context, the workings of her entire life and freedom fell subject to one man's personal opinion.

"I want to ensure you are capable of providing a beneficial and nurturing environment for your children. It would be remiss of me to do otherwise."

She pressed her lips together, glaring at the floor. Her thoughts instantly commenced picking apart his words. *Capable*. Meaning not her own ability, of which he apparently believed all women to be bereft, but the presence of resources she could call on to provide for her. *Beneficial and nurturing*. This her mind translated into being composed of a set of morals which the doctor approved of as proper and good.

Off to the side, a third occupant of the office shifted in his seat. She considered blinking up at him but decided she hadn't the strength. Dr. Mathews, a young man who'd arrived at the facility several weeks after her confinement. As yet, he retained the vivid color of life in his face, a testament to his recent arrival.

Adele could no longer claim such a luxury, the reflection she sometimes caught sight of in windows as she passed stared back pale, with dark circles forming under her eyes. No, the new doctor's tint made him an anomaly in the facility, and she envied him this uniqueness as she felt herself slowly blending into the monochrome of the building.

If he'd been in residence at the time of her arrival, she might have found a reason for hope or attempted to nurture an alliance. New to his trade, Dr. Mathews wore a kind expression and appeared to genuinely wish to aid in the recovery of his patients.

Alas, that moment passed Adele by within the first two weeks of her stay. After her second failed interview with Dr. Garrison, the severity of her situation took root. No matter how she responded to the man's questions, his doubts lingered. She considered simply not responding, but that was unlikely to aid her cause. Sighing, she prepared to repeat the same words she had been, the only words her mind formulated despite her best efforts.

"How do you plan to set up house when you leave here, Mrs. Monroe?" He began, never looking up from the file in front of him.

"I plan to return to Coral Cottage and set up with my children and housekeeper as we had been." If she could locate Bessie. She had no idea what had become of the woman and hoped at least her mother-in-law retained her to help with the children.

The doctor pursed his lips. He appeared no more pleased to hear Adele repeat the same responses as she was to voice them. "And what sort of work do you intend to take up to support the household?"

"Respectable work which aims to uphold my moral character and set an acceptable example for my children."

He gave a harsh sigh. "Do you believe it essential for a mother to be in the home and available for her children?" He weaved his fingers together atop the desk in front of him and fastened a look on her which demanded an appropriate response.

"As much as possible given financial constraints, yes."

His lips flattened into a severe line, the surrounding skin going a shade paler than it already was. "And what is your opinion on women's involvement in greater civic duties?"

Throughout the inquisition, she'd felt Dr. Mathews' observation keenly, finally giving way to the draw and raising her chin to catch him in her periphery. The man reminded her of her initial meeting with Mr. Alderman in the realty office, those fishbowl eyes struggling to emit some unknown piece of information. Dr. Mathews' eyes shone admittedly more congenial, but no more clearly in their discourse.

"I believe women are equally capable of participating, whether through lending voice on a topic or taking up active roles in their local municipalities."

Dr. Mathews' eyes shifted to Dr. Garrison's pencil as it scratched across her file. He needn't have frowned, Adele knew by now her answer was incorrect. But what could she do about it? The doctor asked her opinion, and she gave it.

"Thank you, Mrs. Monroe," Dr. Garrison mumbled, seeming none too pleased with her as he continued to write. "Dr. Mathews, would you please ring for Nurse Davies?"

"Yes, sir." The younger man rose, attempting a reassuring smile in her direction as he passed by.

"I shall review our sessions yet again, Mrs. Monroe, in search of areas where we can make adjustments."

With the interview at an end, nothing remained but for the three of them to sit in uneasy silence until Nurse Davies arrived to escort Adele back to her room. A clock ticked loudly on the mantle, out of sync with the ongoing scratching of pencil on paper. Adele still felt Dr. Mathews' gaze directed at her, but her chin drooped once again to her chest, eyes fixed on the floor. An eternity later, Nurse Davies arrived, and Dr. Garrison looked up from his work.

"Please see Mrs. Monroe back to her room, Nurse Davies." The Doctor instructed.

On that cue, Adele pushed herself up from the chair and shuffled toward the matron. Dr. Garrison's voice sounded as they passed through the door, directed at Dr.

Mathews. "As you no doubt observed, the poor woman persists in a clear case of..."

Nurse Davies clicked the door shut and marched down the hall, expecting Adele to follow.

∼

"Nurse Davies!" Dr. Mathews' voice hailed them in the hall near the large community dining room. Adele's guide halted, turning back to the doctor with an instant softening of expression. Being young and kindly, and good-looking if Adele took the time to think on it, the man had secured instant popularity among most of the staff in the ladies' ward.

The doctor jogged up to them, bestowing a warm smile on the matron. "I'm terribly sorry to interrupt your work, Nurse Davies."

"No trouble at all, Doctor," the nurse insisted. "What can I assist you with?"

"I'm getting ready to interview the new patient from yesterday, but I'm afraid I wasn't able to locate the transfer files. Might you know where they went off to?"

Nurse Davies furrowed her brow a moment and the doctor made use of the distraction to send a glance toward Adele. A moment later, the nurse shook her head. "I'd wager Nurse Styles misfiled them, I swear I don't know how that girl passed her examinations. I can check for you at the orderly desk. When do you need the papers?"

The doctor colored slightly and cringed. "In about fifteen minutes."

Nurse Davies' eyes rounded, and she clasped her hands in front of her, darting glances in both directions down the hall. One way led to the orderly desk, the other to Adele's room.

"I'm happy to keep watch over Mrs. Monroe if you're able to take on the search," Dr. Mathews offered. "I would hate for you to have to make a secondary trip on my account. Especially since we're still so relatively close to the desk." He raised his brows, taking on the irresistible quality of expression one would expect from a puppy or small boy.

The woman debated another moment, then gave a curt nod. "If it's where I suspect, I should only be a minute." With that declaration, she hurried down the hall.

"I'm sorry to inconvenience you, Mrs. Monroe." The doctor angled toward Adele and apologized the moment Nurse Davies rounded a corner, though Adele suspected the task he created was a ruse.

"I'm sure I'll adapt," she attempted a smile.

"Try not to let Dr. Garrison dash your hopes, Mrs. Monroe," he advised in a lowered tone, leaning slightly to facilitate her hearing.

"Forgive me, Doctor, but that's easy for you to say, isn't

it? You are able to go home every day. I am imprisoned here against my will, kept away from my children, and have no earthly idea how to convince Dr. Garrison of my sanity." Surprised by her own declaration, she shot her eyes up in concern, thankfully meeting only a sympathetic gaze in return.

The doctor glanced up and down the hall. "Modern medicine has advanced a great deal in its knowledge of the mind, as well as the management of these facilities. However, there are still a great many difficulties to overcome. Dr. Garrison is a practitioner of the old guard, but you must believe he has your best interests in mind."

"Must I?" she challenged. "Do you believe I ought to be forced to remain here?"

The young doctor shuffled in place much like her son did when confronted with a question whose answer might result in his punishment. "I believe in the validity of your statements, Mrs. Monroe. I come from a large, and primarily female, family. I have two sisters and a fiancée all active in the local suffrage chapter."

"How ever do you get on with Dr. Garrison?" She wondered aloud.

"I suspect he is not wildly enthusiastic to have me as his assistant at present, but as long as I manage not to overtly contradict him in patient treatment, he has no direct reason to complain of me." He sent her another encouraging smile.

"In that case, how can you abide your employment

here?" Adele wondered. "It sounds as though you don't agree with the doctor's methods."

"I believe his methods are somewhat outdated, perhaps, but he has a strong and positive reputation in his field. One lesson I've learned from following the efforts of the suffragettes, is that change takes time."

"Time is not something I feel I currently have, Doctor. My children are growing more each day without me." An aching took up in her chest and she ducked her chin.

"Take heart, Mrs. Monroe. I believe you are well on your way to returning to them."

"How unfortunate, then, your opinion is not the one which holds sway in my release." Adele lamented.

"Perhaps," he furrowed his brow. "You might look upon these interviews as an exercise in discourse."

Adele looked up at him, puzzled.

"You already understand Dr. Garrison has not found the information he is looking for in your current responses." He clarified. "Is there a way to reframe them without feeling as though you've lost the integrity of their meaning?"

She furrowed her brow, considering his words. She certainly couldn't lie about her beliefs, no matter how tempted she was. Given Dr. Garrison's world views contrasted so heavily with hers, she doubted any room for compromise existed.

"After all," the doctor added, "Isn't it better to steer clear of a storm when we see it coming?"

Adele blinked at the man, his words eerily familiar. She opened her mouth to respond, but an angry screech drowned out the words before she could give them life.

Startled, they both turned toward the sound, the wailing of a resident digging in her heels against the attempt of a nurse to tug her down the hall. Dr. Mathews took a step toward the commotion, then remembered his task of guarding Adele. She gave a nod and stepped in that direction herself.

CHAPTER 16

"I won't go, I won't!" the hunched little woman wailed, her stick-like arms amazingly resilient against the pulling of her nurse. "I have to take care of the baby, there's no one else to do it!"

"Oh, you and that baby of yours," the nurse growled through clenched teeth as she struggled to maintain her grip on her ward. "For the last time, there is no baby and you have to get back to your room."

"I won't!"

Another nurse hurried toward the drama from further down the hall. Adele paused when she and the doctor approached close enough that she could remain seen but out of the way. Dr. Mathews stepped up beside the nurse but addressed the patient.

"Why good morning, Mrs. Taversham," he beamed, placing a hand lightly on the woman's arm and nodding to the nurse to let go. The nurse sent a scathing glare toward her ward but complied. The woman, gray hair and eyes wild, stared at the doctor a moment before recognizing him and softening her stance.

"How are you this morning?" Dr. Mathews continued when she didn't answer.

"Oh, perfect, the nurse hissed at her companion as she arrived, neither of them taking note of Adele. "He's going to encourage her again. I wish Dr. Garrison would dissuade him from such behavior. Completely unprofessional."

"Oh, Doctor," Mrs. Taversham grinned. "I'm so happy this morning! Did you hear the good news?"

The doctor put on an exaggerated look of surprise, his eyebrows nearly disappearing into his hair. "No, Mrs. Taversham, do tell." He angled toward the far end of the hall and tucked the old woman's hand into the crook of his arm. The pair looked prepared for a stroll through the garden.

"I had a baby last night, the most darling little angel, you must come by and see him!"

Adele stifled a gasp. A baby? The woman must be eighty years old if she were a day!

"A baby!" The doctor brought his free hand up for emphasis, never pausing his small steps down the hall. Adele realized this woman must have escaped from the more restricted wing around the corner. "That *is* cause for celebration. Congratulations, Mrs. Taversham!"

"You'll come by, won't you? I'm sure you've never seen such a perfect little cherub!"

The nurses followed behind, the first with her arms crossed in front of her. She made no attempt to hide when she rolled her eyes. Adele could likely have made her way back to her own room unnoticed but followed along out of curiosity.

"Of course, I will," Dr. Mathews assured the patient. "I wouldn't miss the opportunity."

"Oh, wonderful," she patted his arm, walking beside him without any sign of hesitation. "Oh!" She halted, sending a wide-eyed look of concern to the doctor. "But not too soon. He's sleeping now, you see, we mustn't wake him."

"Very true," the doctor took on a serious air. "He needs his rest to build up his strength." He looked down at the woman as though seeing her for the first time. "Come to think of it, so do you. Why don't you let Nurse Abel here take you back to your room and get you settled for a nap?" He turned toward the trailing nurses, indicating the second, far kinder in expression, nurse. "I'll be by about lunch time to check on you both."

The woman, looking somewhat confused, as though she'd forgotten something, turned his words over before responding. "That would be fine. Thank you, Doctor." She allowed the young nurse to take her by the arm and direct her. The elder nurse stomped along behind them, glaring daggers all the while.

Dr. Mathews turned back to find Adele staring at him. He rejoined her with a somewhat sheepish grin.

"You must at least admit this is an interesting facility to take holiday in."

"I'll admit it," she gave a half nod, "though I wouldn't go so far as to call this a holiday. What did she mean, she had a baby? Is she truly out of her senses, then?"

"By traditional standards, yes," the doctor acknowledged. "But..." He tilted his head to the side, shoving his hands into his pockets. "Hers was not an easy or a privileged life. She sustained a good deal of hardship and created this fantasy of hers many years ago as a means of comfort. With time and age, she gradually retreated into it so deeply that it is her current reality."

"Her current reality," Adele repeated the words in a near whisper, mulling them over. "Is there no hope of reversing the movement?"

"That's just the question, isn't it?" he shrugged. "There are those who believe we must make every attempt to force the mind into a socially acceptable pattern, others who admit defeat and view patients like Mrs. Taversham as a lost cause, but as for me?" He paused to glance back over his shoulder. "I see a woman who has created, by sheer force of will and power of imagination, an internal world which offers her that happiness this life never afforded her. It's real for her. Every morning she wakes thinking she's just had a child and it gives her boundless joy. Who am I to take that from her?"

The rapid clicking of heels on tile announced Nurse Davies' return. The woman approached, color heightening her cheeks but smiling triumphantly. In her hand, she gripped a file folder, which she saluted the doctor with as she neared.

"My dear Nurse Davies, you are invaluable," the doctor praised. "I thank you for going to that trouble."

"No trouble at all, Doctor," she responded on a somewhat belabored breath, swiping a wisp of hair away from her face.

"I'd best be on my way, then," he nodded, turning back toward the office hall. "Wouldn't want to be late reporting to Dr. Garrison." Nurse Davies gave a knowing roll of her head. "Thank you again. And take heart, Mrs. Monroe," he offered a parting smile. "You are making excellent progress."

Later that night, long after the lights had been turned out and the last of the restless souls quieted their murmurings, Adele lay awake, unable to come to terms with her thoughts.

...A woman who has created, by sheer force of will and power of imagination, an internal world which offers her that happiness this life never afforded her.

Was that what Adele had attempted with all her jumbled thoughts of dreams and reincarnation? Creating a separate reality because she must have been more unhappy than she'd known? But how could she truly be unhappy in a life shared with her children? Dared she consider the entirety of her interaction with Captain Daniels a figment of her imagination? She scrunched her eyes shut and dug the heels of her hands into them. Perhaps this unhappy incarceration would prove a blessing in disguise, preventing her from becoming another Mrs. Taversham.

Impossible! Captain Daniels was most decidedly not a product of her imagination. He used far too many words and phrases unfamiliar to her. And the book! A new fear took hold of her, catching her between regret at not having seen her promise through and horror at the thought someone might find the manuscript and use it as further proof against her sanity.

She rolled to her side with undue force, caught the edge of her blanket in her fist and tucked it up under her chin. A cold draft slithered through the room from the window and she shivered. No matter what answer she considered, she failed to find a solution which might serve to free her.

~

THE NEXT MORNING dragged on interminably, Adele still battling to understand Dr. Mathews' advice. Eventually, she admitted defeat, allowing her mind as much of a rest as she could muster as she awaited the next mealtime.

A knock sounded at her door, catching her attention. She looked up from her perch on the edge of her bed, laying the book Dr Mathews had lent her, with Dr. Garrison's approval, across her lap. The shawl across her shoulders sagged and she reached to set it back in place. Despite the snow having melted away, an icy undertone lingered in the crisp air and what movement she could manage in the small space did little to improve her comfort.

Nurse Davies entered with an envelope. "A letter for you." She handed over the missive, which Adele snatched with abbreviated thanks, and faded again into the hall.

Over the weeks and months Adele formed an appreciation for her mother-in-law's letters completely contrary to her former feelings toward them. They were shorter and farther between than they had been, but that might be more a factor of the screening process Dr. Garrison employed. Most residents received no mail at all, but Dr. Garrison deemed Adele stable enough to interact with carefully curated missives.

This parcel included notes from her children. Blinking back tears, she read them both in turn, her eyes returning multiple times to the segments which tugged at her heart the most.

...Grandmother says you're getting well, please do so faster! I miss you!

...It's dull here and so stuffy, when can we return to the house at the cove?

...I've found a magnificent book! It's all about pirates and treasure and islands in the tropics! I don't think Grandmother likes me reading it, but because it was father's and our tutor said I need the practice she let me keep it. I think I should like to be a sea captain. But I suppose I can't be because who would look after you then?

...Grandmother is forever scolding me for ruining my dresses, but the ones she gives me aren't properly made! She won't let me climb trees or go out when it rains. We've been cooped up all winter!

The words blurred, a hesitant smile hovering on her lips. She allowed her hands to drift with the letter back to her lap, turning her head in search of the muted light entering through the window. Images of the past weeks flitted through her mind, heightening her anger at the injustice of her predicament until she shot to her feet.

"All right," she mumbled to herself. "Adele has failed at her task. Where is Adira?"

She began pacing the room, running through each of Dr. Garrison's questions in turn and examining her responses. She brought to mind every self-assured justification and argument she could recall Captain Daniels making during their arguments. What was so different in how he phrased things? How was it he always managed to win the argument? Very often convincing her she agreed with him in the process.

Invigorated by her children's words, she soon lost track of the time, refusing to join in the midday meal when the nurse came to fetch her. The sun faded into darkness and the naked bulb hanging from the ceiling blinked to life. Still, she paced. With no pen and paper at her disposal, she repeated thoughts and phrases as she landed on them, maintaining and building upon those she deemed useful and casting aside the rest. Even the dimming of the light at bedtime failed to dim the energy inherent in her cause. She was determined not to sleep until she'd solved her dilemma. Indeed, she stared into the darkness until the sky began to brighten yet again. But when at last she shut her eyes in the frightful stillness of that hour before the dawn, she did so with a smile.

For the first time in weeks, she looked forward to her next interview with Dr. Garrison.

CHAPTER 17

"Dr. Mathews informs me you've shown a marked improvement in enthusiasm and participation in your sessions with him, Mrs. Monroe," Dr. Garrison took his seat at his desk. "And I must say I've also noted an improvement to your general mood. Might I ask the source of this sudden change of heart?"

Adele sat up in her chair and beamed at the doctor, hands folded primly in her lap. Dr. Mathews sat in a chair off to the side, she acknowledged him with a smile as well.

"Doctor," she began, focusing her most sincere and innocent expression on the man, "I feel so foolish, and am quite embarrassed by the amount of your time I've wasted."

"Is that so?" he asked. "Please elaborate."

"Dr. Mathews encouraged me to give your questions sincere thought and ensure that my responses to you are a true representation of my beliefs."

"Did he now?" The doctor shifted his eyes sideways in Mathews' direction, but did not turn his head. Dr. Mathews raised a brow at her from where he sat, chin in hand.

"He did," Adele nodded. "And once I did so, I realized I haven't been at all clear! No wonder you've been concerned, Doctor, and how very right of you to be so."

"Well," the doctor straightened in his chair, puffing his chest slightly. "I'm certainly encouraged by your show of confidence, Mrs. Monroe. Rest assured, your stay here, however much you may have felt inconvenienced by it, is a show of dedication to your wellbeing."

"Oh, I understand that now, Doctor."

Twisting his features into what almost sufficed as a smile, Dr. Garrison opened the file in front of him and took up his pencil. "Are you ready to begin, then, Mrs. Monroe?"

"Yes."

"I think we ought to revisit the question of your home life with your children upon your release."

"Yes, that is exceedingly important." Adele nodded in agreement.

"How do you plan to set up house when you leave here, Mrs. Monroe?"

"I intend to return to my home with the children and

our housekeeper. It would be best, I think, to keep in constant contact with my late husband's family until I can ascertain the viability of selling and perhaps returning a bit nearer to Boston." She pursed her lips and nodded. Ascertaining the viability of these activities did not denote doing them. And she could very well find the options not viable or another possibility preferable.

"That's a far cry from your previous plan, Mrs. Monroe," the doctor eyed her with a hint of suspicion.

"Not really, Doctor. You see, my initial intent in buying the home was to provide a stable place for my children to grow, but do you know in all this time I have been so focused on my own circumstances and what I'd thought best, I didn't properly consider the needs of my children."

She ducked her chin, twisting her hands in her lap. "Rather shameful of me, wasn't it?" She looked up, hoping to convey how sincerely stricken she was. "The letters I received from them the other day awakened me to the fact and I am now wholeheartedly committed to ensuring their needs are met."

And those needs currently include searching for pirates and treasure along the shore in a quiet and wholesome small harbor town.

"A commendable exercise in self-examination, Mrs. Monroe." The doctor's pencil began a harried march across the file. Dr. Mathews remained silent, but his eyes reflected a hidden smile.

"And what sort of work do you intend to take up to support the household?"

"I've made a re-evaluation of my annuity, simple mental calculations which will require further work, mind you, but I believe there are a few areas in which I can improve upon my household economics." *Should I choose to deprive myself and my children, which I am not likely to.* "There are also still several pieces of furniture and decor in the home from the previous owner which might fetch a price." *Should I choose to sell them, which I am also not likely to do.* "Between those two adjustments, I believe I could stave off the necessity of outside work long enough to consider more permanent solutions."

"And what might those be, Mrs. Monroe?"

"Forgive my impertinence, Doctor, but I believe you will also ask about my views about mothers being available for their children at home?"

"Yes..."

"Well, as mentioned previously, I do believe mothers should remain home as best as possible." The doctor set down his pencil and observed her. She swallowed but did not shrink into her chair. "I realized when I thought again about our first interview that I'd allowed my grief over losing my husband to deter me from considering remarriage. For the sake of my children, I think I ought to re-examine that possibility."

Which required no promise on her part to take action on such a course.

"Very forward thinking of you, Mrs. Monroe." Dr. Garrison relaxed in his chair. Dr. Mathews took a slouched position of necessity to cover a widening grin.

"That leaves us with only one more question, Mrs. Monroe. What is your opinion on women's involvement in greater civic duties?"

"I maintain that women are every bit as capable of participating in such as their male counterparts."

The doctor's pleasant mood dulled and Dr. Mathews furrowed his brow. Adele enjoyed a moment of internal victory before continuing.

"However, what I belatedly understood from this question, Doctor, is that you actually mean to inquire about whether or not I would personally participate in such activity, isn't that right?"

Dr. Garrison straightened, gawking at her. "Well, yes, of course—"

"And shame on you, Doctor, for not being clear. You see I've just proven how sadly incapable I am of swift thought, which I am sure is a necessity of such work." She shook her head in a mildly reprimanding manner. "No, I could not imagine taking on such responsibilities and have never had any inclination to do so."

That was true. The functioning of the greater world around her was something Adele gladly left to others who maintained a true interest in such things. She had enough to do caring for herself and her children.

"Well, I, ah…" Dr. Garrison shuffled the paperwork in

her folder, picked up his pencil, then set it down again. "I am utterly amazed at the depth of progress you've managed in such a brief period of time. You see you only wanted for the clarity of a breakthrough, and one never knows how much time that might take."

Adele nodded enthusiastically. "You were quite right to keep me here, Doctor, I might never have made these connections otherwise."

"Mind, we'll have to observe you a brief while longer to ensure the permanence of your recovery," the doctor warned, closing her file. "But I think it safe to say you may begin preparing for a return to your familial home."

Adele couldn't suppress her smile or the happy tears welling in her eyes. "Thank you, Doctor!"

"Dr. Mathews, if you would?" Dr. Garrison tilted his head toward the switchboard.

"If you don't object, sir," Dr. Mathews responded, "This is my final assignment for the day, I am happy to escort Mrs. Monroe back myself and save Nurse Davies the chore. She must be in the midst of preparing for change of shift."

"Yes, you're quite right. Very well then." Dr. Garrison flapped his hand at the two of them and Adele hastened to exit with Dr. Mathews.

They walked in companionable silence until they'd left the office hall and were well ensconced in the residential hall.

"Congratulations, Mrs. Monroe," Dr. Mathews smiled

down at her after a glance to ensure they wouldn't be overheard. "That was an exemplary performance."

"It wasn't a performance, Doctor," she insisted. "I only did exactly what you recommended."

"Indeed, well you comported yourself in excellent fashion. I am sincerely impressed by your show of confidence."

"Thank you."

They reached her door, and she took a step over the threshold, turning back to the doctor. "Thank you for all your help, Dr. Mathews. I am certain you will be a tremendous positive influence on your profession and wish you well in your career."

"Encouraging words I will hold dear through the more difficult portions of it, thank you. And for you, I wish you a swift return to normalcy and many happy days spent with your children."

She moved into the interior of the room as the doctor shut and locked the door. A bright blue sky beckoned from the window, and she made her way over to examine it. Reaching her hands up to the ledge, she stood on tiptoe to observe what she could of the tree branches outside. The brittle limbs swayed in a chilled breeze, but something unique in the movement caught her attention. A flash of color. She tilted her head and waited as the branch passed again through a particularly bright ray of sunlight. There it was again. A flash of green. The first new buds of spring making their debut.

CHAPTER 18

Coming home to Coral Cottage played out like a dream, though Adele struggled to label it either positive or negative. The house itself remained untouched, everything exactly as she'd left it. Mr. Alderman, receiving word from Bessie that Adele had taken sick while visiting Boston, took it upon himself to maintain the yard in her absence, so even that remained familiar. The children shouted their glee at returning home, running immediately down to the shore in search of treasure. Even Bessie, a woman not at all prone to sentimentality, sighed and smiled upon entering the kitchen.

For Adele, however, for as much joy as the house gave her, she found bittersweet memories in every corner and infusing every object. At first, she harbored a secret hope the captain might have ignored her dictate to leave. She sat in the chair beside her fireplace and her eyes wandered the table beside her for an ornate lamp shaded with stained glass. She shut her eyes and took in a breath, realizing her nose searched for a trace of tobacco smoke. It was maddening. All the more so because she didn't dare give vent to her distress, her freedom too new and fragile.

The worst of it had been opening the drawer of the davenport desk and finding the captain's manuscript. Fortunately, that same memento which threatened to tear her heart asunder provided her the distraction she needed to settle into her life again. She decided to fulfill her promise. Staying up late to complete revisions, she threw herself into finding a publisher for the anonymous work she would peddle as having been written by a friend. To her great relief, she found the note on which she'd scribbled the name of a publisher Gregory mentioned.

In the end, her desire to be rid of the manuscript and her guilt overcame her fear of visiting the publisher and all proceeded smoothly. The work was accepted, marketed to rave reviews, and the royalty checks promised to provide Adele with a healthy income for the rest of her days. Surely now she would feel herself at ease and begin her life anew.

How foolish human hopes can be.

Springtime settled resolutely over the whole of the cove, insisting upon rapid change and movement. Flora bloomed and fauna stirred from their winter slumber, the fishing trawlers competed with the return of small merchant ships for space at the docks, and the sleepy town awoke to the excitement inherent in the promise of warmer weather.

Except for Adele. Wandering a perpetual fog of half-contentment, she took to wandering in reality, often during the day when the children were off to school. She walked wherever her legs directed her, paying little heed to her direction. She often found herself near the harbor or at the docks.

That's where she strayed one blustering day in late spring. A storm had passed through in the night, leaving the docks still sodden as the sun battled to assert itself through stubborn dark clouds. They growled their discontent, threatening to unleash another torrent. The wind twisted Adele's skirts about her, pushing her toward the edge of the pier, but she hardly noticed. She only clutched her shawl tighter about her shoulders.

The fine hairs at the base of her skull prickled a warning. Tourists and general gawkers were never all that welcome on the pier, especially when a merchant ship attempted to load and unload its stores along the small space. She inched a step closer to the pier's edge, her one concession. The movement proved ineffectual in helping her escape the uncomfortable crawling of her skin warming under the unseen gaze.

She set a small, gloved hand atop the wooden pillar

beside her, eyes searching the choppy, green-hued waves while her mind wandered. "Captain..." the whisper dissipated, never quite forming a tangible remembrance, the remaining words held captive in a constricted throat. A chilled breeze misted her face, and she welcomed the excuse for rapid blinking and a shiver.

Behind her, the noise of the docks continued. The crew of a merchant ship that had docked in the night swarmed and scurried about, busily unburdening the ship of its cargo. Had she considered it, Adele might have thought it a curious sight. The ship loomed larger than those normally docked in the small harbor. Also, had she taken better note of her surroundings, she might have detected the subtle changes in tone from one moment to the next as the drama of daily life unfolded at her back.

She did not catch any of those things, however. Therefore, she remained oblivious when the shouts of instruction became shouts of concern. Her ears did not discern the instant the straining of ropes transitioned to a series of loud snaps. Even the crash of barrels against the planking followed by ominous rumbling initially went misfiled by her mind, attributed to the darkened sky. Only when the warped planks beneath her feet began to tremble did her instincts awaken and compel her to turn.

Her eyes widened as she realized the severity of her position. The shipment in all its components rolled toward her from every side, the first of the barrels already reaching the edge of the pier and hurtling over. She'd lost the opportunity to avoid them, could only attempt to lessen the impact by presenting her side and putting up her arms to shield her face.

Immense pain shot through her leg and hip an instant before she flew into the sea, hitting the water at an awkward angle and knocking the breath from her lungs. She managed a partial gasp, her mouth filling with salt water as she began to sink. Despite the season, the day called for a heavier woolen ensemble which proceeded to soak up the icy water with frightening swiftness.

She struggled briefly, only managing to further entangle her legs until they became useless. Her arms alone stood no chance of counteracting the weight of her clothing. The sea darkened around her, and a strange calm began to settle over her. Somewhere from the depths of memory, she recalled the captain assuring her he'd wait for her until the end of her lifetime. She stopped struggling, allowed the water to take hold of her, pull her into its embrace.

Something hooked about her waist, tugging brutally upward. The motion revived her sense of self, and she attempted another bout of resistance, but it only tightened the vice around her waist as her lungs burned and darkness overtook her vision.

A moment later frigid wind slapped at her cheeks

demanding she rouse herself, but she only lolled her head against the unknown buoy keeping her afloat. Her ears rang with ambiguous shouts and noises, a dozen more hooks and vices took hold of her, raising her in an unsteady mass and setting her down on a hard surface. Head heavy, vision still dark, she let go of the noise surrounding her and sank deeper into herself.

Something rolled her from side to side, a harsh tugging at her clothing began, accompanied by the distinct rip of sodden fabric. Painful pounding at her back. Then a warmth and pressure at her lips, but she hadn't the time to wonder at it as a sudden influx of air to her lungs incurred protest from her body. Angry gulps of salted water churned and gurgled their way up her throat, causing her to sputter and gag. Another roll to her side and pounding on her back, but she remained too engrossed in coughing to protest the abuse.

Soon her breath returned, albeit in short rasps, and the blackness faded incrementally from her vision. She attempted to open her eyes, only to scrunch them closed again against the brightness of the day. A shadow fell over her and she attempted opening her eyes again to find a rough silhouette against the sky.

Blinking, she waited for her vision to clear, revealing as it did so blues eyes as deep and stormy as the sea gazing down at her. Eyes encased in a familiar face. The face of a Nordic seafarer, chiseled by salt and ice, with golden beard and cropped hair. His hair wasn't light and neatly combed back as she remembered, but dark amber from being drenched, and falling over a lightly lined forehead. She blinked again, fighting against the darkness still pulling at her awareness. His lips moved, the same strong mouth, but slightly different.

She couldn't hear his words, only watched as she might a moving picture show. A droplet of water formed at the tip of one golden lock plastered against his temple, then rolled its way down across his cheek, pausing at the hollow, unable to make the leap alone, waiting for the next droplet to join the journey and tumble down to her.

A loud chattering disrupted her jumbled thoughts, causing her irritation. Had she not been so disconcerted by the vision before her, she might have realized her teeth were the cause of the chattering, or that the instability of her vision resulted from the involuntary tremors and convulsions attacking her musculature. But her cognition extended only as far as bewilderment at the portrait come to life before her.

The figure looked away, reaching an arm out to some unseen companion, his profile silhouetted against the too-bright sky.

"Captain Daniels." the words escaped, unable to bear another moment locked in the addled questioning of her mind.

The portrait stilled, deep blue woolen coat dangling

from his hand. Restoring his attention full to her, his eyes squinted, the lines at their corners deepening.

For some unknown reason it warmed her. Foolish, such a foolish fancy. She wanted to laugh at herself but hadn't the energy. At best, the corners of her mouth twitch upward, but the effort proved too much, and her mind retreated into the comforting depths of unconsciousness.

∽

A GENTLE ROCKING soothed Adele in her dreamless slumber, teasing her awake as she used to do with her children when they'd napped too long. Warmth surrounded her and she burrowed into it, rubbing her cheek against something with the characteristic roughness of wool. A familiar fragrance tickled her nose, salt, tobacco, and a new, sultry hint of sandalwood. She started, twisting about in her cocoon and becoming entangled. Pain worsened the experience, her entire body registering complaint against her movements.

"Calm yourself, you're perfectly safe," a low voice rumbled like a storm on the horizon, beautiful at a distance, menacing if one wandered too close. A voice so hauntingly familiar, yet new to her.

Adele stilled, concentrating on calming her breath and focusing her bleary eyes. The wooden walls around her were awash in the warm amber glow of lamplight. On the wall beside the bed she lay in, a shelf sported several books oddly covered over by netting. Beside the shelf a round window with metal frame revealed a star-laden night sky. The horizon swayed and she realized she lay aboard a ship. Turning, she sucked in a breath and froze as a stab of pain shot through her side.

"Steady," the voice warned. "You've been mightily trampled and have the bruises to prove it. Nothing broken, though, luckily enough."

That voice. She must see its owner. Random images floated across her mind. The docks, the sea, Captain Daniels' portrait in her parlor. But it wasn't his portrait, it was more vivid. Curiosity flaring, she continued her shift in position, one tiny, agonizing movement at a time. By the time she completed the task her breath came in heavy gasps, and she felt ready to sleep again.

The man sitting at the open davenport desk nearby watched her with his head tilted and wearing a half grin. He rested one elbow on the edge of the hinged writing surface, a book dangling from his hand. A lamp with the wick lowered glowed from the internal portion of the desk. And his features. Nearly identical to those her mind recalled from dream. But it couldn't be...

"That was a grand endeavor," he noted. "What motivated you to such an undertaking?"

"I wanted to see you."

"I'm flattered, but you ought to rest. It's extremely late or, more accurately, very early."

Her memory hadn't tricked her. The man, assuredly a flesh-and-blood man, presented the image of Captain Daniels. She narrowed her eyes at him. Something was different in this man, but she couldn't tell what. "Why aren't you resting?"

"For the simple fact, Madam, that you are currently occupying my bed. While under different circumstances I might not object to such an arrangement, current events render me inconveniently and uncomfortably berthed.

More memories surfaced. A commotion on the pier, sinking into the sea, something pulling her out again. "Oh dear! I'm sorry!" She squirmed again, attempting to sit up and letting out a small yelp when her muscles complained.

"Here now, belay that!" the man tossed the book on the desk and stood, taking a step in her direction. Adele calmed and lay back on the pillow. He observed her a moment longer, eyes narrowed, before returning to his seat. "I see I must take additional care with my pronouncements until you've come further to your senses."

She looked about the room again, belatedly understanding his words and her surroundings. "Good heavens, how long have I been here? Bessie and the children! They don't know where I am, I must get home!"

"Confound it, Madam!" he roared when she again looked as though she might try to sit up. "Calm yourself." He rose again, setting his broad, tanned hands to her shoulders and pressing her back into the pillow with astonishing gentleness. "Your housekeeper is aware of your current status. She came to town with all the subtlety of a hurricane in search of you as evening encroached and raised a holy clamor." He crossed his arms in front of his chest, but remained beside the bed, apparently not convinced Adele would refrain from movement. "I would gladly have allowed her to abscond with you, but the doctor suggested you ought not to be moved until after he's seen you in the morning."

He paused his tale long enough to place the chair closer to the bed and sit. "She tried to argue staying with you, but I would be da—," he cut off the statement, shifting in his seat. "I am put out enough having one female aboard my ship, I won't stand for two. It took my personal vow to take up the task of night watch myself before she relented."

"Well," Adele smiled at his sullen ramble. "I am grateful to you, Captain..."

"Erickson."

"Captain Erickson, I take it you were the one to rescue me?"

"If by *rescue* you mean fish your foolhardy form out of the sea, yes, that was my misfortune. Da—" again he caught his expression. "Freezing water this time of year." He concluded with a grumble.

"Damned freezing," Adele agreed, cheeks flaring.

The captain raised his brows, but his eyes sparkled. "Such language is unbecoming of a lady."

"Quite right. Please use it at your discretion to prevent me from being tempted to."

"Very well," he nodded, putting Adele at ease, as though some great wrong in the world had been righted. "Now returning to our conversation. Why, might I ask, Mrs. Monroe, were you prowling about the docks amid the active turmoil of ships loading and unloading?"

The feeling of being watched came back to mind and her color heightened, though she hoped the dimness of the room masked it. "You were watching me," she asserted. "But how did you even know I was there? So many people were moving about the pier."

He stiffened his posture. "I believe you have circumscribed the question, Madam."

A temporary battle of gazes ensued, but Adele relinquished precedence to his question. "An unwise decision on my part, I admit, but I was... not feeling myself and hardly took note of my surroundings."

"That much was clear. Did your Captain Daniels play a part in this loss of self-perception?"

Her eyes widened. "That is forward of you, sir."

"It is, my apologies. However, the name did come up and I wish to ensure all notable parties are aware of your condition if you deem it necessary. I assume, as you have had no additional visitors, that your housekeeper has informed your husband of your whereabouts.

"My—" Her color deepened as she caught his meaning. "I am a widow."

A brief show of surprise crossed his features, perhaps also a hint of relief. "My sympathies. And this Captain Daniels?"

She studied him, considering his persistence and wondering how she ought to answer. "Is also not who you presume him to be. My home was once his, but the captain died nearly two decades ago. There resides a portrait of the man in the house, you bear a striking resemblance which surprised me."

He pondered her response for an extended time before returning his attention to her and no doubt noting her heavy eyelids. "Mrs. Monroe, if you wish to expedite your departure in the morning, I suggest you return to your rest."

She did not wish to either expedite her departure or return to her rest, but silently acknowledged her weariness with a nod.

"Is there anything you require?"

She took breath to respond in the negative but paused. "Would you entertain a foolish request?"

"That depends on how foolish. My sympathy for your plight has its bounds."

"Have you ever sailed the fjords of Norway?"

His eyes widened. "Yes."

"And seen the northern lights?"

"Of course."

"Describe it to me?"

He hesitated, perhaps wondering if the fall into the sea addled Adele's head. Nevertheless, he relented and began weaving a tale of wonder, mystery, and enchantment which soon lulled her into a deep and restful sleep full of enthralling dreams.

CHAPTER 19

Adele might have slept the entire morning away if not for the arrival of the doctor and Bessie. Between the two of them, no chance existed Adele might prolong her stay in Captain Erickson's quarters. A fact which undoubtedly cheered him, though it caused her a small pang of disappointment. Sleeping in the maritime rendition of her bedroom while docked in her local harbor constituted the closest she'd yet come to sailing the world and she would have enjoyed prolonging the daydream.

"Thank goodness you're sound, Miss!" Bessie proclaimed as she bustled into the room, shutting the door on the nose of the doctor, who would be made to wait until Bessie deemed her mistress suitably prepared for company. "I didn't sleep a wink all night for worry. Not one wink!"

She set about unpacking a basket of sundries she'd brought along, as well as fresh clothing. Once she sorted through her supplies, she assisted Adele to a sitting position, propping her up with the pillow.

"I suppose we ought to leave off dressing you until after the doctor's seen you," she muttered to herself as she filled the wash basin and plucked a washcloth from the assortment of items in her arsenal. "But we can at least get you into your own shift. I've got a shawl for you too."

"My own..." Adele looked down at herself, noting an unfamiliar garment. It looked to be... A man's shirt! "Good heavens, Bessie! What am I wearing?"

"One of the Captain's shirts," she tsked, shaking her head. "I argued with him for taking such liberty before the doctor could even arrive, but I won't say he didn't have the right of it. From what I heard you were so blue there was nothing for it but to get you completely dry and tucked into a warm bed."

"Do you mean the captain... That I was..." She hid her face behind her hands, mortified.

"That you were, and yes he did," Bessie verified. Then, completely out of character, she gave a girlish chuckle. "Might have been a good sight more enjoyable for the both of you had you been awake. He had to get changed too!"

"Bessie!" Adele gaped at the woman.

"Beggin' your pardon, Miss, but I've got eyes too and

they surely like the look of that man." She hurried on before Adele could admonish her. "Have you noticed he looks a bit like that portrait in the parlor?"

"I... haven't really seen him yet," she shrugged, lowering her lashes.

"Well, once the doctor commended him for his fine and swift care of you, I had to relent a bit. Especially seein' as to how he was still shivering from the swim himself and had no bed to curl up in."

"Oh dear," Adele moaned, peeking between her fingers at the now vacant chair beside the davenport desk. The writing portion had been restored to its closed position, the lamp nowhere to be seen, possibly secured inside the desk.

"As said, nothing to do about it now. Here, take this across your shoulders. I'll have your hair pinned up in less than a minute and we can let that impatient doctor in." Bessie handed Adele the shawl and set to work tying her hair up in a simple bun.

When Bessie nodded and turned to allow the doctor entry, Adele reached for what she assumed was a blanket crumpled and forgotten at the side of the bed. In actuality, the piece turned out to be a dark blue woolen peacoat. A memory came to mind of Captain Erickson reaching for something as she lay on the pier. Then when she woke in the night, the scratch of wool at her cheek.

"You are looking a considerable sight better this morning, Mrs. Monroe!" the doctor greeted her, glaring at

Bessie as he shuffled past. The short, heavyset man wore wire-rimmed spectacles and a kind smile meant to encourage reciprocity. He walked up to the bedside and set down his bag. "You caused quite a stir yesterday, quite a stir," he noted, searching his bag to procure a stethoscope. "Lucky the captain spotted you and reacted swiftly."

"Yes, so I gather," she responded as the doctor pressed the flat disk of the instrument to the upper portion of her chest. He signaled Bessie to help her lean forward, then repeated the process at several points along her back. Once she was set back against the pillow again, he took her wrist between his fingers and plucked a watch from the pocket of his vest.

"You've recovered admirably. I worried you might take a fever." Refolding his stethoscope, he returned it to his bag. "I'd like to take a quick look at your right leg, as that's where the most injury occurred, but other than that I see no reason not to allow you to be moved to your home. Once there, however, I advise you to remain in bed until I come see you tomorrow. By then I'll be assured of no more serious or lingering damage to your leg and will give instruction for your further recuperation."

"Thank you, Doctor."

Once the man left, Bessie reverted to her flurry of activity and quickly set Adele to rights, ensuring she was properly dressed and outfitted as though she were about to go for a stroll. Unfortunately, the illusion dissipated the instant Adele made to exit the room and put weight on her battered leg.

"Oh!" she stumbled, reaching for the chair and lowering herself into it. "Bessie, I don't think I can walk as far as the door. How are we to get home with me in such a state?"

"I've taken the liberty of seeing to that," Captain Erickson materialized in the doorway, looking incredibly dashing in a simple ensemble of dark navy trousers, high-necked shirt and a coat. His polished brass belt buckle glinted, and his captain's hat sat at a rakish angle atop his head. Doffing said cap, he entered the room. "I've arranged for a car to take you home and will send one of my men to see you get properly settled once there." He announced. "I can assist you from here to the car myself if you have no objections." He held out a hand.

"That's very good of you, Captain, thank you." Adele accepted his hand and pulled herself upright, resting heavily on her uninjured side. She expected him to come up beside her and assist with her hobbling, so prepared for the potential slide of his palm around her waist to help support her. She enjoyed all of two seconds of pride at her excellent forethought before he shocked her by not only setting a hand about her waist but bending to sweep her completely off her feet!

An instant later they were in motion, the captain maneuvering swiftly and expertly along the decks of the gently swaying vessel. He paused at the gangplank only long enough for Bessie to catch up and precede them down to the car waiting on the pier.

Adele clutched at his shoulders, breathless, and stared at his lapel. The man proceeded as though not in the least inconvenienced and gave no sign of discomfort related to the burden he carried. Meanwhile, Adele's heart attempted to beat itself senseless against her ribs. That intoxicating scent she'd only ever caught phantom whiffs of enveloped her. Warm salted wool, sandalwood and tobacco…

Then all at once the heady, reassuring presence of him receded as he set her into the backseat of the car and released her, stepping back and securing the door. Bessie took the seat beside her, and a tall, very sturdy looking young man joined the driver in front.

"Feel free to call on me for any further assistance you might need while my ship is in port. I'm happy to oblige." The captain asserted from where he stood beside her window.

"Thank you again, Captain," she nodded.

With a final nod and touch to his cap, he signaled the driver they were ready to proceed.

⁓

Two days later saw Adele lounging on a chair in her garden. The temperature had warmed enough that if one stayed in the sun, it was actually quite comfortable and relaxing.

Not that Bessie approved of her spending extended time out in the spring air, but now that her muscle aches had subsided enough for her to hobble independently with a cane, the woman was unable to restrain her non-compliant mistress.

Aside from that, she could no longer stand to lay abed in her room. Not only was she bored out of her wits, the space reminded her too much of too many things. Bad enough when only the memory of Captain Daniels permeated every fiber in the room, but the similarity in construction to Captain Erickson's quarters ensured *that* man remained forefront in her mind as well. Upon waking this morning, she declared she would go mad if she didn't get some fresh air to clear her head.

"Miss, you know the doctor said to be careful of catching a chill, you ought to be inside." Bessie clucked as she backed through the kitchen door carrying a tray laden with coffee and pastries.

"It's a beautiful day out, Bessie, and I feel perfectly fine. I wasn't in the water that long after all." She made light of her recent scare for Bessie's benefit. The woman hovered constantly, and Adele feared the near drowning coupled with her recent prolonged stay in Boston created a phobia in the woman of ever letting Adele out of her sight again. Adele appreciated it though. When she allowed herself to ponder the events herself it inevitably ended in a great deal of fear and anxiety. Especially when she recalled the horrid stillness of the sea as it pulled her into its depths. She gave a small shiver.

"There, you see!" Bessie leveled her with a stern look. "You're cold, you ought to go inside."

"Nonsense, I'm not cold. Here, I'll put my shawl back on if it appeases you."

"It does not," she grumbled. Pouring a cup of coffee and setting it within reach.

Bessie looked about to continue her argument when the doorbell sounded. "Here, now, who could that be?" She grumbled, not pleased at being interrupted in the midst of her tirade. She bustled away, leaving Adele to smile at her receding form.

She rested her head against the back of her chair and closed her eyes. Her mind wandered to the topic which preoccupied her most in recent days. Captain Daniels. She wondered what had become of him. His disappearance was no more or less than what she'd asked, rather what she'd insisted upon, but it proved difficult to imagine a world without him now that she knew the alternative.

And what of Captain Erickson? The resemblance, both in looks and mannerisms, was far too uncanny. Yet the captain had been so adamant during their last conversation about reincarnation. He wouldn't have changed his mind... Done something so irrational and risky... That wouldn't be like him at all.

"You've got a visitor, Mrs. Monroe," Bessie called from

the back door. Adele looked over to see her housekeeper beaming with glee. She was about to ask for further explanation, but saw it for herself an instant later when Bessie held the door for Captain Erickson. Another shiver traveled over her from head to foot as she watched the man approach.

"Forgive the intrusion, Madam," he pressed his fingers to the brim of his cap with an abbreviated bow. "I took it upon myself to inquire after your continued recovery, but will endeavor not to demand too much of your time. I see I've interrupted your refreshments." He gave a nod to the tray and her coffee cup.

"Not at all, I've barely begun." She smiled up at him, unable to counteract the intense happiness seeing him inspired. "You are welcome to join me if you have the time."

"That's a fine idea," Bessie broke in. "I'll just take this," she commandeered the tray, "and set space for you both *in the parlor.*" She smiled, retreating into the house before Adele could contradict her.

"Rather insubordinate sort, that one," The captain noted.

"Only in my best interests, I assure you," Adele responded.

"May I escort you inside?" he offered a hand.

"Thank you." She reached for her cane, then his hand, her stomach somersaulting when their palms met.

He tucked her hand into the crook of his arm, and they proceeded slowly inside.

The portrait over the mantle caught his attention as they entered the parlor, Adele noted the hitch in his step and the way he stared at the piece, but made no commentary, seeing her comfortably settled before moving to inspect the portrait more closely.

"Is this..." he pointed at the work.

"Captain Daniels," she confirmed. "Not the most skilled portrait, but I hope you can see now why I mistook you."

"Yes, you're right on both points. A dismal rendering, but the resemblance in certain features is uncanny." He shook his head and joined her at the sofa with a thoughtful expression.

"Is this your first visit to our sleepy little town, Captain?"

"It is. An odd coincidence..." he hesitated, furrowing his brow. "Though I find myself no longer believing in such a thing..." He shook his head. "Forgive me, Mrs. Monroe, You must think me deranged, but I swear I am not ordinarily so tongue-tied."

"I shall take it as a sign of my awe-inspiring presence effecting you." *Goodness*, and she was not ordinarily so forward.

The captain chuckled, the sound moving through her like a ripple in the sea. "You would not be far from the truth." He sipped his coffee while considering his next words. "You know, I had no reason to come to this port. A small harbor, easily overlooked, yet it drew me. For years I had it in mind to find a reason to dock here. Now that I have..."

The nape of Adele's neck began to prickle, and gooseflesh erupted along her arms. "You feel as though you know the place, don't you?" She breathed.

His eyes found hers, searching their depths as though she guarded all universal truths. "Yes, but how can that be?"

She swallowed. "The world is full of oddities, Captain, but I would not worry over a happy sentiment toward a locale."

"Where it just that, Madam, I would not mention it at all, I have often felt a similar familiarity with ports as diverse as those in the southern seas of Asia or the Norwegian Fjords you inquired about." He set down his coffee and turned to face her fully, the light in his eyes causing her lungs to contract.

"The trouble is," his voice took on a low, hushed quality and he leaned in close to her. "I also feel as though I know you. From the moment I saw you wandering the pier, my mind told me I must know you somehow. And here you sit, your lovely eyes wide as though you've a ghost sitting before you. Now tell me, how can that be?"

Her head swam from the overexertion of her heart, her pulse rushing in her ears with the same deafening insistence she experienced once before. "Not the ghost of a man, Captain," she whispered, suddenly lightheaded. "The ghost of a dream." Her eyelids drooped heavily, and she swayed forward in a swoon.

The captain caught hold of her, lips pressing against hers as a matter of necessity, arms wrapping about her securely. The parlor edged out of her awareness, and she found herself suspended in the captain's embrace above a shimmering pool of water. A silent seaside cavern surrounded them, the trickle of water from the tunnel above frozen in time.

"Captain?" She blinked at the familiar face she hadn't seen in so long.

"I'm here with you, Adira. I cannot be without you."

A subtle shift and Captain Erickson gazed down at her, the two faces masks of each other. She smiled. A wide, genuine smile of joy which broke the spell and sent them both diving into the pool below. Sparks of gold and silver erupted behind her eyelids, and she pulled back with a gasp.

Sitting in her parlor once again, Captain Erickson's arms about her, she stared wide-eyed at a countenance just as wild and uncertain as hers must be.

They sat in silence, struggling for breath and unwilling to unclasp their hands, though they returned to a more respectable separation otherwise.

"Mrs. Monroe," Captain Erickson began after a

prolonged silence, "May I have your permission to pay court to you?"

A smile broke across her features. "You may, Captain Erickson. Captain?"

"Yes?"

"What is your given name?"

Color suffused his cheeks, and he cleared his throat. "Gregory."

Her smile widened. "I shall endeavor to use it."

EPILOGUE

"You've been at that desk for hours," Gregory admonished as he entered the captain's quarters from the outer deck. "I have half a mind to have it tossed overboard, and that would grieve me sorely as I paid a hefty sum for it."

He walked up behind Adele where she sat at the desk, still scribbling feverishly in the new leather-bound journal he gifted her. Resting his palms on the edge of the desk to either side of her, he bent to place a lingering kiss at the juncture of her neck and shoulder. The pen in her hand stilled and she leaned her head to the side to help facilitate his actions.

"It's just that I have so much to say," she responded breathlessly, letting the pen slip entirely from her grasp. He kissed her cheek and straightened, leaning against the desk to look down at her as she continued her justification. "Each day manages to bring so many new wonders. I don't want to forget a moment of it."

"And yet you've lost half a day at this desk," he teased, leaning forward until they were cheek to cheek. "And half the morning for sleeping in, he whispered near the curve of her ear.

"I believe that was your fault for having kept me up so late last night," she flushed hotly, feeling delightfully wicked in her teasing and not at all ashamed of the memories which sprang to mind.

"I take only half the responsibility, my dear, but now," he tugged at the chair to turn it away from the desk and moved around behind her again. "I must insist you pause your chronicling temporarily." His arm came up at her side, a length of fabric in his hand. Before Adele could ask, he'd already wrapped the cool silken sash over her eyes. "I have a surprise for you."

His hand cupped her elbow, prompting her to stand and leading her through the room. The door latch slid out of place and the hinges creaked. A draught of crisp air kissed her as they walked across the deck, hinting of ice and misted with salt. Sounds of the crew's daily functioning amplified from the muffled noises she'd heard in the background while seated at the desk. Men tossed quips and instructions at each other across the deck or between deck and rigging. Ropes tightened, chains clattered. Water lapped against the hull and the mast creaked.

She took note of that sound in particular, wishing to find the best description for it. Several renditions already graced her journal, none she was completely satisfied with. Gregory had a mind to either replace the ship or go into an early retirement when they returned home, his beloved sails having long since become obsolete. He admitted to uncertainty regarding his ability to adapt to a steam powered ship. He had some experience with them, but never enjoyed them quite so well as the older ships. They both agreed only sails would do for their honeymoon voyage.

Piercing through the now familiar sounds came the happy shouts of her children. They had taken to the excursion the moment they set foot on the ship, running about the decks, following crew members, and asking unending questions. The men didn't seem to mind, taking the assault in stride. Gregory insisted seamen were essentially a motley group of large boys who all still shared most characteristics of children. Even so, Adele attempted to maintain a schedule of activities with them to keep them out of the way.

After a short walk, Gregory paused, setting her hands on the ship's railing and returning to a stance at her back. She tilted her head in question.

"A moment of patience, he chuckled as his fingers moved to the silken fastening at the back of her head. The blindfold slipped away, and she blinked her eyes open, then gasped in surprise.

Above her, the night sky was alight with flowing rays of color. Greens and blues, pinks and purples, shimmered across as far as the eye could see, their glory reflected in the sea. Adele brought her hands up to her mouth while Gregory circled his arms about her waist. She leaned her head back against his shoulder. The lights shone in abstract shapes, sometimes a straight cut across the stars, other times in serpent-like curves. As she watched, absorbed in the beauty of it, the colors appeared to take delight in their audience, waiving and dancing, pulsing and receding.

"Oh, what a magnificent sight!" She sighed, dropping her hands to her chest as tears stung her eyes.

"One of many I hope to show you."

So entranced was she, she didn't notice one of his hands slip away to his pocket, nor its reappearance at the periphery of her awareness, until again something cool and smooth slid across her collar bones at the base of her throat. Reaching a hand up, her fingers settled on a string of something perfectly round and smooth. "Pearls?"

"Could there be anything else for a captain's wife?" He returned his hands to her waist.

She smiled, leaning into him once again. "In what exotic port did you find them? Japan, no doubt, their pearls have become quite popular."

"No, these are far finer in my opinion, natural, not farmed, and a nod to the Arab divers who collected them in generations past."

"Arab?" A faint alert sounded in her mind. A memory buried somewhere in the recesses.

"Yes, it was the oddest thing. We docked in Bahrain to collect Oriental trade goods. I was enjoying a bit of shore time wandering the markets when a young boy ran up to me and began tugging at my sleeve, insisting that his grandmother wanted to speak with me. I attempted to send him off, assuming him a miscreant of some sort, but he persisted fiercely.

"Seeing the boy would not relent, I gave in to curiosity. He led me to a home in the old quarter of the city where a woman of perhaps sixty years sat mending out front. The woman took one look at me and disappeared into her home, returning a few minutes later with these pearls."

"How very odd." Adele breathed, breaths shortening as her heart quickened pace. She turned in his embrace to face him.

"I agree. But when I refused to take the pearls, she shoved them into my hand, proclaiming I must give them to the love of my heart, that she might recognize me as the love of hers.

"Thereafter she promptly shut the door in my face and would have nothing more to do with me. I still have no idea why she singled me out, but— my dear, are you all right?" His amusement vanished and he looked to her with concern. "You've gone quite pale. Let me bring you back inside."

"No! No, it's all right, I'm fine, truly." She endeavored to smile and look chipper, though from his expression she must have failed. "I just... This all still feels like a dream. Such a wonderful dream. I'm afraid I'll wake one day, and it will all be gone."

"You needn't fear, my dear, our dreams are our only true reality. We always find our way back to them."

"I think I'm beginning to understand that." She rose up onto her toes to press her lips to his, ignoring the catcalls from his crew and the noises of disgust from her children. All that mattered was the exuberance of spirit which ignited in her, reflected in the joyful play of kaleidoscopic color in the cosmos above.

The End

Author's Note

I don't recall exactly how young I was when I first saw the 1947 film version of "The Ghost and Mrs. Muir," but it cemented Rex Harrison as one of my top girlhood crushes. I discovered the film at least forty years after it released and would not realize an original novel existed (written by R.A. Dick/Josephine Leslie) for at least another twenty. I'd continue with my unearthing of the 1968-70 TV series, but I'm already feeling aged by all these decades. Suffice to say, this story has been an ongoing obsession.

Though I've always loved the bittersweet nature of this romance, the thought of *what if* always nagged at me. What if Lucy and Captain Gregg could have had a happily ever after during her lifetime? Once I became a writer, and after reading a couple of irritating paranormal romances which magically materialized a ghost into flesh for the sake of a love scene then dematerialized him again, I decided why not put my own fan-fic spin on this classic and see if I can be a bit more creative.

Now, don't get me wrong, I put it off for a long time. I didn't want to cause upset to anyone who, like me, already loved the original. But I genuinely wanted to try my hand at showcasing love and romance as more than physical interaction. We allude to it all the time in romances, yet I noticed this message getting lost in some paranormal stories. I may have failed at my task, but at least I gave it a shot, right?

I focused most on the dialog between the ghost and the widow. I hate to admit it, but I don't think I would have loved the original without the cantankerous commentary of the captain. The author laced in the most beautiful hints of love and caring so seamlessly; I didn't want to lose that in my version. Given the difficulties inherent in a single point of view (Lucy's), this artistry of dialog made the story stand out in my library as an eternal favorite.

There are a few additional themes I wanted to mention while we're chatting. You may have noticed I tried to stay true to a very general original plot, veering wildly off course with the introduction of Theosophy and asylums. These were completely based on my own interest and curiosity.

I want to state that I have no negative opinion of the Theosophical Society. In fact, I find its views remarkably interesting. My Mr. Fairly (Dr. Harris) is every bit as selfish as the original, his association with the society an unfortunate circumstance of this writer's imagination. The topic was simply one I had a desire to read up on.

Next, there is of course the theme of reincarnation. This again is a personal point of curiosity, but I felt it meshed well with some of the conversations of the original. I love the way the captain tries to explain some of the inexplicable properties of the universe to Lucy, only to conclude there are no suitable human words for it. The Theosophical Society offered a perfect segue for this theme, as I could think of few other options to introduce this eastern belief into an early 20th century western society tale.

And then there's the asylum. I recalled learning at some point these institutions held a reputation for being excessively cruel and often used as a dumping point for unwanted family members. I did find some intriguing information on that front, but alas, much (not all) of this reputation had been corrected by the timeframe of my story. This was probably good for my purposes, as I have a tendency toward the dramatic in my books. Even so, I liked the backdrop as a place for Adele to work through her own doubts about life and her relationship with Captain Daniels.

Overall, I tried to combine my favorite snippets from previous renditions of this tale and add in a little of myself to the mix. I hope you enjoyed it! If so, please remember to leave a review of this book on your site of choice (amazon, goodreads, etc.) to let me know. Alternatively, you can find me via the contact information listed below. If you enjoy backstory details, also look me up on YouTube, where I try to share the best historical bits and bobs I come across in my writing.

Wishing you long hours of happy reading,
Emilee

I hope you enjoyed reading this story as much as I loved writing it for you! You can always find all of my books, plus additional works, on my Amazon author page, amazon.com/author/emileeharris

Be the first to hear about new books and updates via my newsletter, which you can sign up for at http://authoremileeharris.com/ or send a note to emilee@authoremileeharris.com

Currents of Love

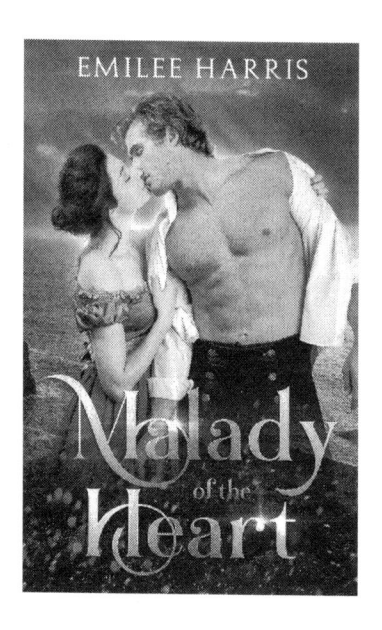

When this sailor discovers a delectable stowaway on board, will he turn her over or keep her for himself?

A woman unlike the rest...

Lady Amaryllis Langdon is not meant to be a bride. Her tomboy ways, once amusing to her family, have long since become an embarrassment. What's worse, she knows the man she loves, her twin brother's best friend, will never find her desirable. When her elder brother arranges a match for her, she realizes her only chance at acceptance requires leaving those she loves and setting out to find her own place in the world.

A man of noble heart...

The only thing that has kept Gavin MacAllister, Baron of Dailemor, from professing his love for lady Amaryllis, is the knowledge her brothers would never approve the match. Her engagement shatters his last hope, convincing him to take a position as a ship's surgeon in the Royal Navy. When he discovers the ship's powder boy is actually his lady in disguise, he must wage war against both their wills to see her safely home... And into the arms of another.

One click MALADY OF THE HEART today!
https://books2read.com/u/bQ6zJv

MALADY OF THE HEART
SNEAK PEEK

Hampshire, England 1811

The clang of metal striking metal echoed across the courtyard of Heathermoore Manor as Gavin MacAllister, Baron of Dailemor, lunged to the side, blocking his opponent's saber at the last moment. The move put him at a disadvantage. He'd held up well to this point, but the awkward positioning made it difficult to regain his footing. The weakness did not go unnoticed, his opponent charging in with renewed vigor. A chuckle escaped amid the harsh breathing and gasps emanating from behind the fencing mask in front of him, the mesh concealing glittering blue eyes that always took immense pleasure in besting him. A corresponding upward tilt tugged at the corners of his own lips. Another flurry of advances met by Gavin's increasingly desperate attempts to parry culminated with a triumphant "Ha!" as he felt the blunted edge of the sword drag across his side.

"You're forever leaving that flank unprotected." Came a soft feminine voice directed at him amid short gasps. His opponent removed her mask, allowing dark tresses to tumble down over her shoulders in stark contrast to the white sparring uniform. The sight set his senses to reeling every time, which went a long way to explaining why he continued to voluntarily showcase his sub-par fencing skills.

"My long-acknowledged Achilles heel," he conceded as he removed his own mask. "In a true encounter you'd best stay to that side of me if you wish to maintain your second.

Amaryllis Langdon, Mary to Gavin, smiled brightly, stealing the breath Gavin had nearly recovered as she set down her equipment on a side table and walked toward a dining area where refreshments had been set out. The courtyard overlooked an immaculately kept garden boasting an assortment of roses and an excellent selection of medicinal herbs. The latter were added at Mary's suggestion when Gavin announced his intent to study medicine. As children, when the Langdon siblings visited his own estate of Dailemor, it was Mary who stayed in the kitchens with him, his mother and their cook, preparing tinctures, teas, and various remedies. The twin sister of his best friend, Mary's eager engagement in every activity managed to capture his curiosity while they were still young, at some point superseding her brother in his affections, not that she knew it.

He blinked at the memories, mirroring her movements and setting aside his sword as he observed her swiping damp tendrils of hair away from her face, his fingers itching to do the work for her. A pitcher of minted water provided a distraction as he poured her a glass, but the fleeting moment evaporated with the first enticing movement of her throat as she swallowed. Bowing, he indicated a seating area of intricate ironwork ensconced by a wisteria trellis. The attempt at propriety cost him, as the trousers and one of her brother's old shirts she wore for these fencing matches did little to hide her curves from his view as she preceded him.

Somewhere along the way during their acquaintance, their games of pirates and adventure on the high seas lost the veneer of innocent imagination. These matches, taxing as they were on his emotions, helped to maintain some of that childhood excitement. The realities of a nation at war and the responsibilities of adulthood had tainted their old amusements, but he couldn't manage to decline her continued invitations to practice as her brothers did. There was something so heartfelt in the way she looked at him. It made his own foolish heart's suffering more than worth the price when he saw her eyes light with a smile after he agreed.

"I do wish you could stay longer at Heathermoore, it's dreadfully boring here with all my gentlemen gone to their careers," Mary shrugged and sighed at the mention of her brothers.

"My dear Mary, you can't tell me you didn't know this day was coming. You Langdons are a seafaring lot. Your brothers were born with brine in their veins, and I daresay there's a goodly amount of it in yours as well." Gavin grinned as Mary rolled her eyes. The elder two brothers had followed in their father's footsteps, heading to the naval academy and off to sea as soon as their parents would allow it. The youngest, Eric, aspired to the same, but life intended otherwise for him.

"True enough, but is it my fault I haven't a man's freedom to chase the winds and explore the world as I see fit?"

Gavin couldn't argue with the bitter observation. The Admiral had been indulgent with his children, even the girls developed a taste for the sea, though none so ardently as Mary. She'd scuttled up the netting and shadowed the sailors of her father's ships with as much enthusiasm as her brothers when their father was in port, her sisters preferring to wax poetic about the beauty of the waves and listening to stories of mermaids and vast underwater kingdoms. Unfortunately, Mary suffered for it. There came a time when her family no longer approved of her traipsing about with the boys and tried to insist she conform to a proper life indoors.

A sadness washed over her as she gazed out over the gardens, dimming the luminous nature he so enjoyed.

"Come now, lass," he admonished, reaching over to crook a finger under her chin, "I have every faith ye'll find yer own gateway to adventure." He let his Scottish brogue slip into his words, a noted indication of the level of ease between them, and his heart skipped a beat when she tipped her head to let her cheek brush his hand before pulling away to sit up in her chair.

"We're nearing thirty, my friend. Time may herald maturity and opportunity for a man, but it advances no favors for women." The tartness in her tone compounded with the years.

"A man of intelligence will have no hesitations—"

"The only man who understood me is at the bottom of—" she gasped and clapped a hand to her mouth. "Forgive me, Gavin. I know I shouldn't—" she cut the statement short, shaking her head.

When she turned from him to hide her tears, he forced himself not to reach out to her. Her father wasn't the only man to understand her, but as a lowly Baron with no hope of securing her affections he had no right to make that assertion or provide consolation.

"We all grieve in our own time, lass," he offered instead. "Your father was a good man and your greatest admirer. Holding to your dreams holds him to your heart, I imagine."

"That's exactly it!" She sent a cheery smile his way.

Though Admiral Langdon also encouraged Mary to behave as society required, it pained him, and he often assuaged his eldest daughter with trips to the docks and conversations on naval strategy. His sudden death in the Battle of Trafalgar had all but shattered the family. Life resumed in more muted colors and tones, nothing quite as enjoyable as it had been. At times Gavin wondered if she didn't feel out of place in her own family and felt a strong pull to bolster her spirit, so full of tenacity, creativity, and life. He wondered how her family couldn't see it as something to be nurtured.

"Have your sisters not won you over to the benefits of needlepoint and dancing, then?" He meant it as a light-hearted transition away from the memory of her father, but the insensitivity of the words as they hit his ears caused him to cringe.

A hint of remorse colored her cheeks. "They're wonderful, of course, but surmounting the gap between myself and my sisters is, I fear, an impossible task. I'm closer in age and temperament to all of my brothers, but I've tried their patience for me." She reached her hand across the table to pat his arm, sending a shock of heat through him, her palm leaving a tingling sensation in its wake, "You've been the one constant and unwavering joy in my life, Mr. MacAllister, please excuse my selfish desire to horde you away. You have been quite like a brother to me as long as I can remember."

She beamed that dazzling smile at him again and he

ground his teeth, forcing himself to return the gesture. His affection for the angelic creature before him held nothing of brotherly intent. It shamed him to admit it, and he dare not do so outside of the innermost fantasies of his heart. The change occurred with such subtlety he truly could not say how long this torturous malady had lain upon his heart, but with each encounter and the passing of time he began to doubt of ever finding a cure.

Marching steps across the marble tiling alerted them both to approaching company. Gavin sat further back in his chair, then chided himself. He'd developed a habit of moving away from Mary in a guilty fashion when her brothers were near, yet his sense of propriety was not so addled he should have any need to do so. The group of them had been fast friends since childhood, for goodness' sake. He looked up to see Mary's two elder brothers, Daniel, now Earl Langdon, and James coming toward them, Daniel with a weary scowl and James with an arched brow and half smirk directed at him.

~

"Ammy," the family pet name drug out with the strains of a weary sigh as Daniel approached. He wore his naval uniform, hat tucked under his arm, and Gavin didn't miss the scowl of disapproval he sent toward the fencing equipment on the side table. Mary's elder brother, and the head of the household, had strict ideas of propriety which intensified after his father's death. Censure loomed in the once carefree household, often falling on Mary for her interest in hobbies afforded almost exclusively to men.

Even so, the family enjoyed their time together and Mary didn't look forward to her brother's upcoming departure. He would return to his command within the week after completing repairs to damage his ship sustained during its last skirmish. Daniel paused in front of Mary, his hand wandering to the edge of his uniform coat, tugging to smooth any wrinkles his movement might have caused. Even if the war were over, Gavin imagined the man would continue to wear the uniform out of habit alone. "I'm sorry to interrupt, but I need to speak with you. Will you come to the study?"

Mary's brow furrowed slightly, but she stood to follow her brother. "Yes, of course. " She turned toward Gavin, a warm glow suffusing her features, "Mr. MacAllister, It was a great pleasure to host you here as always. I hope we will see you again soon."

Having also risen, Gavin issued a polite bow and forced his eyes not to linger in her wake as she and Daniel left the courtyard.

James took up residence in Mary's vacant seat, snatching up a sandwich and leaning back. "Do tell me you managed to best her this time, old man, she's become a positive nuisance with her superiority complex." He surveyed his sandwich with inordinate care, propping one ankle over a knee, but his tone held a hint of amusement.

There was no use feigning he didn't notice or understand the cause for his friend's humor. In a foolish move years ago, Gavin once admitted to his feelings for Mary. Teenagers at the time, Mary was preparing for her first season. Gavin threw a fit when he thought about it long enough to realize what that meant. She might marry. Some other man would hold her and care for her. The extent of his worry over the issue at the time still caused embarrassment. James found the whole situation hilarious for some time, but eventually took a more reticent view, not wanting to continue his best friend's embarrassment or cause any grief for his twin.

The turning point came when Gavin announced he would ask for Mary's hand himself. The ill-planned announcement convinced James of Gavin's earnestness and necessitated the uncomfortable task of explaining why his family wouldn't consider Gavin a suitable option. A painful lesson, but one Gavin had to learn to avoid causing Mary any social harm. He crawled back to his station and rebuilt the wall he thought their friendship had taken down.

"I am at the singular disadvantage of a lacking education. You know it was all my family could do to send me to Eton with you, fencing lessons while outside of those hallowed walls were not on the docket." He sent his friend a half smile and placed a morsel on his own plate despite his lack of appetite.

As a Baron, Gavin had never been on par with the Langdons and was surprised when James took him under his wing after arriving at school fresh from Scotland, but the family never took his rank into consideration when inviting him into their home. Previous kindness notwithstanding, he understood from his earlier experience the same courtesy would not be extended where the daughters of the house were concerned. He sometimes wondered if he might have won over the old Admiral, but Daniel was a different story. The man understood better than any of them their title had been hard won, and considered it part of his duty to ensure the family continued to rise in social standing, marriage being an optimal way to achieve that goal.

"The open flank?"

"The open flank."

"I'm of the impression you must be allowing her to win these matches. How can you possibly continue to leave your side unguarded after all the mock deaths you've suffered through the years?" James chuckled as he shook his head.

"I wish I could justify your statement, but it would seem my younger years in the highlands froze whatever portion of the brain dictates that particular self-survival mechanism."

"You sound uncertain, sir doctor."

"The brain is not a well-documented organ, my friend, I admit to having encountered few of them during my apprenticeship."

"In either the dead or the living, I presume."

"I respectfully refrain from comment."

James burst out laughing. "The gift of your wit will be sorely missed around here, and I daresay I'll not find its like aboard my new assignment if my brother is any indication of the seafaring humor."

"He does appear particularly strained of late." Gavin noted, thinking back to the increased moodiness the Captain showed during this leave period.

"Something's got him flustered," James nodded, his brow furrowing. "But he's tight-lipped as ever, and if mother is aware of something, which I suspect she is, she's not alluding to it."

"Best to leave it be, sounds like."

The conversation paused, each of them content with his own thoughts, before Gavin caught on to something James had said. "You've been assigned then?" He turned to his friend with genuine interest. Passing the exams to become a lieutenant was difficult enough, but gaining placement aboard a ship was practically impossible, despite the current need for officers.

"I have indeed," James confirmed with a grin. "I report at the docks first thing next week."

"Congratulations, my friend. I don't doubt you're

planning a celebration before then?" He tossed a knowing grin James' way.

"I am indeed, and don't think you're getting out of it! I intend to set out with you to Liphook. The inn serves an excellent ale."

"Mm-hmm," Gavin turned to ponder a set of small birds chirping and hopping along the courtyard tiles, hiding his smile in a sip of water. "By the hand of a lovely wench who, as I recall, delights in leaning over just a bit too far when she pours for you."

"I'm sure you must be mistaken," James mused, then, sitting up straight in his chair and nailing Gavin with a determined look, "And what of you, friend? Have you given any thought to my offer?"

Gavin pressed his lips together. "James, I've told you, I appreciate it, but I haven't the draw to the sea that all of you inherited. Becoming a ship's surgeon when I can fulfill the same calling on shore holds little draw."

"You say that now, but you have no idea how dull life will be with all of us Langdons missing from the landscape. Daniel and I are off to our ships, Eric is engrossed with another of his clandestine assignments, and the young misses are forever twittering on about dances and concerts and who knows what else."

That Mary was left out of the tally was not lost on Gavin, but bringing her up would only cause awkwardness in the conversation, so he bit his tongue. "You mean how peaceful it will be? True, I may find myself at a loss, but Mr. Eldridge has plans to retire his practice, at which point I'm sure to be put to good use."

"Mr. Eldridge has been threatening retirement for at least the last decade! You can spare a few years. Besides, you'll gain valuable experience along the way."

It wasn't the first time the topic had come up, but James seemed adamant about it of late. Gavin wasn't sure what his friend was up to, but the change in demeanor made him uneasy. "Why don't we take one assignment at a time." He tipped his head back to note the position of the sun in the sky. "If you have a desire to sample the ale at the inn, we'd best get ready to go. I doubt the innkeeper will be generous if we wake him."

"Well said! I'll meet you in the foyer." He slapped his hand on the table with a smile and hopped up to head back into the manor, leaving Gavin to wonder, tapping his fingers on the table. Unable to rationalize his unease, he stood to follow his friend.

One click MALADY OF THE HEART today!
https://books2read.com/u/bQ6zJv

FREE Download:

Get your FREE copy of The Commodore's Daughter, prequel to Emilee's *Currents of Love* series when you sign up for the author's mailing list at:

www.authoremileeharris.com

Privileged but isolated on her family's estate in Barbados, Ayanna Wilson dreams of seeing the world, but finds herself fleeing both her home and her father's plans for her future instead. She doesn't anticipate barreling straight into the arms of Lieutenant Edwin Langdon, whose mesmerizing blue eyes and unerring sense of integrity spark an entirely different kind of desire. But her exploration of this budding attraction is short-lived when her travels go awry and she finds herself without a friend on a rogue naval ship, her only hope for salvation the handsome lieutenant her father tasked with protecting her... If he survived.

Determined to succeed in his naval career, Edwin Langdon must tolerate the unending animosity of his commanding officer, but when he's assigned to escort the Commodore's family to England rather than participate in intercepting French fleets, Edwin is ready to resign his commission. Then he collides with Miss. Wilson, as beautiful as she is forceful. Intrigued by her strength of character, she sparks a heat in his veins hot enough to rival the Caribbean sun and leave him breathless.

When mutiny sees Edwin thrown overboard and Ayanna taken hostage, Edwin must find a way, with the help of an errant privateer, to take back the ship, thwart an enemy ambush, and win back his Commodore's daughter.

Made in the USA
Columbia, SC
12 May 2025